7-91

THE SEALED KNOT

Also by Elizabeth Law

THE SEALED KNOT

Elizabeth Law

Walker and Company
New York

First published in the United states of America in 1989 by
Walker Publishing Company, Inc.
Published simultaneously in Canada by
Thomas Allen & Son Canada, Limited, Markham, Ontario
Library of Congress Cataloging-in-Publication Data
Law, Elizabeth.
The sealed knot / Elizabeth Law.
p. cm.
ISBN 0-8027-1085-9
I. Title.
PS3562.A857S4 1989   89-9164
813'.54—dc20   CIP

Printed in the United States of America
10 8 6 4 2 1 3 5 7 9

THE SEALED KNOT

= 1 =

THE FAIRFAX DRAWING-ROOMS were pleasantly crowded on this warm June evening, as the blue twilight stole through the open windows to blur the lamplight and the hum of voices mingled with the muted strains of the string quartette in the gallery. In the dining-room a cold collation awaited the guests and there were packs of cards on the baize-covered tables in the library, but for the moment people were content to linger, sipping the wine served to them by white-gloved footmen, the ladies eyeing other women's dresses, the gentlemen eying the ladies.

A slender young lady had evaded her chaperone and was perched somewhat recklessly on the narrow balcony that overlooked the street. Her hair, haloed by the lamplight, was the colour of dark flame, curling naturally over a broad brow that tapered to a pointed chin. Eyes that slanted upwards at the corners, a nose that the critical might call snub, and a mouth that was unfashionably wide combined to give her the aspect of a kitten. Her ball gown, fashioned of some soft, feathery material, bared her shoulders and was tied with a silver ribbon at the high waist.

A gentleman who had just ridden at an easy gait through the park and turned into the crescent of elegant town residences checked his mount and looked up at the railed balcony with quickened interest in his face.

Mounted, he seemed part of the bay he sat—his long legs encased in immaculate white breeches, a caped greatcoat emphasising the width of his shoulders. On foot, he was above middle height, his black hair styled in the Brutus cut above a square, harsh-featured countenance remarkable mainly for a pair of heavily lashed eyes that looked dark in the fading light.

The young lady above him was turned slightly away from where he sat his horse. She'd thrust one slender arm between the bars; the other held onto a strut of wrought iron that supported the lantern over the door. As he watched, she gave a long, most ungenteel whistle and threw something down. Whatever she threw was caught by a tiny, ragged figure, which darted out of the shadows and promptly vanished again.

The man dismounted and swooped down on the ragged figure as the girl above turned her head in a startled manner.

"Lemme go, guvnor. I ain't done nuffin'," a voice whined.

From above the plea was repeated in equally indignant if more refined accents.

"Unhand him immediately, you great bully."

"So that he can make off with the swag you just passed to him?" the gentleman enquired, holding the wriggling figure closer to the light. It was revealed as a tattered and grimy urchin of about ten; male, to judge from its garments. One cheek was distended and one bony hand was fastened tightly upon something.

"He is not making off with it. He is eating it, sir," the girl hissed, now leaning so far over the railing that she was in imminent danger of toppling into the street. "'Tis a beef patty, for it's seldom he gets beef for his supper—when he gets supper at all."

Captor dropped captive onto the cobbles without further argument. Still clutching his patty, the child scrambled away.

"Relation of yours?" the gentleman asked.

"No, indeed. No relation at all," the girl said crossly. "One of my orphans—oh, they are calling me. I'm coming, Henry."

She pulled herself into an upright position, unwound her arm from the wrought iron, and vanished within, taking all the lamplight with her.

"What on earth were you doing out on the balcony?"

The question was posed by a fair-haired young gentleman who strolled up, took possession of her hand, and exclaimed instantly, "What in the world have you in your glove?"

"Crumbs of beef patty. Excuse me while I go and clean it off."

She flashed him a brilliant smile and went rapidly in the direction of the ladies' dressing room, where one of the maids sat with pins, needle, and thread to repair any damage sustained during the more energetic dances. The palm of the white glove was too stained to be wearable. She took one of the spare gloves that had been provided in various sizes and smoothed it over her hand, congratulating herself that she hadn't snagged her skirt on the railing.

Walking along the corridor to the drawing-rooms again she almost collided with a broad-shouldered gentleman who was headed in the same direction.

"Well, well," he observed pleasantly, "it's the beef-patty girl! Are you now going in search of a dessert for your *protège*?"

"I would be grateful, sir," she said with dignity, "if you would banish the entire episode from your mind."

"It never occurred," he said promptly.

"It is only that many people do not realise that there are people within walking distance who have very little to eat," she said earnestly, fixing her gaze on him.

Her eyes were a clear silvery grey, and there was a sprinkling of freckles across her nose.

"You're not a reformer, are you?" he enquired. "There is nothing more tedious than a pretty woman who wants to reform the world."

"Oh, that is a neat compliment couched in a reproof," she said. "I shall keep the compliment and disown the reproof."

She gave him her quick, glancing smile and went ahead of him into the drawing-room, where she was immediately claimed by Henry Fairfax and borne off to the long, narrow ballroom that stretched across the back of the mansion.

"You came in with Simon Adair," Henry said. "Are you acquainted with him?"

"Not at all. You mean the gentleman who came in after me? I didn't notice him particularly."

"No money at all," he said, which in Henry's opinion at least, disposed of Simon Adair as a person of consequence.

Simon Adair was a musical name, with echoes of old romance in its cadences. He had not struck her as very handsome. The blue of his eyes had been unusual—more of a deep turquoise—and when he smiled, his teeth had been blunt and white. Her recollections ended in a yelp as Henry trod on her toe.

"I say, I am sorry!" He stopped short, looking rueful. "I never was all the crack on the dance floor. Shall we take some refreshment?"

"I think we had better." She limped after him into the dining-room, where several people were helping themselves to various items from the buffet.

Simon Adair was there, leaning against the wall and surveying the scene. As Henry fussily helped her into a chair he straightened up and came over.

"Adair." Henry bowed somewhat coolly. "Good to see you again."

"Good to see you and—?" The turquoise gaze lingered on her.

"Miss Harvey," Henry supplied. "I trod on her toe and am now making amends by getting her some refreshments. But you have none."

"I am not hungry," said Simon Adair. "I only came in to count the beef patties."

"What on earth for?" Henry looked puzzled.

"Have you not noticed that the beef patties are the first items on a supper table to vanish?"

4

"Sounds to me as if you're a mite foxed," Henry said. "Much more sensible to eat first."

"Are you going to bring me some food, Henry?" Miss Harvey asked the question somewhat hastily.

"At once," Henry said gallantly and plunged into the group milling about the table.

"I wonder if he will bring you a beef patty," Simon Adair mused. "If he does I can throw it out of the window for you."

"Mr. Adair, it is not very honourable of you to tease me so," she said indignantly.

"Miss Harvey, you must not labour under the misapprehension that I am honourable," he returned promptly.

"You are certainly not a gentleman." Bright colour had dyed her cheeks and her eyes were stormy.

"I give you credit for being able to recognise one," he said, bowing with a flourish that made her stamp her foot in exasperation and immediately wince.

"Did Henry really stand on your foot? You had better let me take a look."

As he was speaking and before she could protest he had knelt down and was tugging off her thin satin slipper, pressing her toes with a grave expression on his face.

"Mr. Adair, what on earth do you think you are doing?" Her cheeks were scarlet now and she made a vain clutch at her skirt as it rode up her calf.

"Checking for breaks and sprains," he said.

"Are you a physician?" she demanded.

"No, but I can tell a broken bone when I feel one. Did you know you have a hole in your stocking?"

"Mr. Adair, unhand my foot immediately!"

"With reluctance, Miss Harvey." He carefully replaced her slipper and, rising, looked down at her with a glint in the turquoise eyes. "Would your Christian name be Cinderella?"

"Sparrow," she said.

"You did say Sparrow?"

5

"Sparrow—and don't dare to make any comments. It was my father's choice and I am very satisfied with it."

"As you ought to be," he returned imperturbably. "So much more original than Amelia or Louise. I would hazard a guess that your father, seeing this tiny, sweet-voiced babe, being himself a lover of Nature in all her glory—"

"He named me after a racehorse he'd won money on," she broke in.

"I do hope I have something you fancy." Henry was returning, bearing two laden plates and two goblets on a tray.

"It seems I must forage for myself," Simon Adair said. "Your servant, Miss Harvey. Fairfax."

"I thought I saw Adair holding your foot," Henry said, setting the refreshments out on one of the many small tables that dotted the room.

"He was looking for broken bones," Sparrow told him.

"I didn't land on it that heavily," he protested.

"He appeared to enjoy holding it," Sparrow said demurely.

"Odd sort of fellow altogether," said Henry, blissfully unjealous. "Can't even recall the mater inviting him. He got sent down from 'Varsity, not that that signifies, since most fellows get sent down sooner or later. Hasn't a bean to bless himself with. Very old family."

Henry was not the most exciting companion in the world, Sparrow reflected, watching him carefully dividing meat from bones. He was very steady and serious for a young man of twenty-five, and there wasn't the least possibility of his squandering the family fortune and driving his parents into an early grave—which showed he would make an admirable husband. Involuntarily she sighed, turning her eyes to where Simon Adair had resumed his place by the wall. There was a glass of champagne in his hand but he wasn't drinking it. He was staring about the room, his brilliant gaze moving from one person to the next, his jaw set grimly. For an instant she had a glimpse of someone vastly different from the man who had flirted with her.

Then his eyes fell on her and the grim look became a raised eyebrow and a teasing smile. She looked down hastily at her chicken in aspic.

"Sparrow, my dear, I've had no opportunity to tell you how charming you look."

Lady Fairfax, one of the latest turbans adorning her head, sailed up graciously. Henry's mother was a feminine version of himself, her features regular, her hair naturally fair, her eyes the same pale, clear blue. In her midforties and with scarcely a line on her face she was fully aware of her consequence in the social sphere and constantly aimed higher.

"Thank you, Lady Fairfax." Sparrow had risen and bobbed the obligatory curtsey.

"Your father is well, I trust?"

Lady Fairfax disapproved of what little she had heard of Justin Harvey, and this prevented her from regarding her son's friendship with Sparrow with unmitigated delight. Being a fair-minded woman, however, she also remembered that Sparrow's mother had been one of the Hampshire Faynes, though from a cadet branch.

"Yes, ma'am, he's very lively for his age," Sparrow said cheerfully.

Lady Fairfax, who knew herself to be a year older than Justin Harvey, winced slightly but retained her smile.

"You must convey my regards," she said majestically. "Henry, may I have a word? I know Sparrow will excuse you."

Her son needed to be reminded there were other girls to smile at and dance with, especially Jane Marquis, whose father could certainly get Sir William a peerage if he chose to exert himself. She was as ambitious for her husband as for her son and would leave no stone unturned to further those ambitions.

"I won't be long," Henry said, and went off, looking faintly miffed, with his mother.

Sparrow hoped that was true. If she sat here for long, one of the chaperones would come and talk to her. Though most of the unmarried ladies had come with a mama or a duenna, there were two or three elderly ladies to keep watch on the rest. Sparrow had suggested that Tizzie accompany her, but Tizzie had refused, saying she couldn't abide to sit and watch the dancing, and Justin had told his daughter that if she couldn't be trusted to behave herself without a watchdog she ought not to attend balls at all.

"Will you stand up with me, Miss Sparrow?"

That man can move as silently as a cat, she thought, jumping slightly as Simon Adair spoke in her ear.

"My foot is still hurting," she said coolly.

"Is that why are you are tapping it on the floor in time to the music?"

Sparrow bit her lip to check her laughter. He was infuriating, and nobody had given him leave to call her by her given name, but in his presence she suddenly felt more alive. It was odd because she was not conscious of having felt less alive before.

"Perhaps you would care to take a turn on the terrace if the idea of dancing doesn't meet with your approval," he said.

"I am not sure—," she began doubtfully.

"We can ask your chaperone to join us."

"Oh, I don't have a chaperone," she said artlessly. "Tizzie thought it would be very boring to have to sit still while everybody else was dancing."

"Tizzie is—?"

Despite her reservations, she had laid her hand on his arm and was moving with him to the steps that led down to the terrace spanning the back of the house.

"Tizzie O'Hara," Sparrow explained. "She is the widow of Captain O'Hara and has taken charge of our household since I was a small child."

"Widow of a sea captain?"

"No, sir, a prizefighter," she told him. "Captain O'Hara was a noted pugilist in his day, but unhappily sustained a fatal injury while battling Wild Jim Bristow, and she became my father's housekeeper."

"Your father is—?"

"Justin Harvey. Mr. Adair, you ask a great many questions."

"I am interested in my fellow men," he replied smoothly.

She remembered the grim set of his mouth as he had surveyed the dancers, as if he sought a certain face in the crowd and not a friend's face.

"My father does not go often into Society." There was a faintly defensive note in her voice. "He spent many years abroad and has lost touch with many people he previously knew. Tizzie regards me as her own child, which is very comfortable since we don't care to correspond with my mother's family."

Not for the world would she confide that her mother's relatives never contacted either her father or herself.

"The truth is," Justin had told her, "that they didn't consider me good enough for your mother. Well, they were right in a way. There wasn't a man living good enough for that girl and I'm the first one to admit it, but they were thinking of rank and quality. When she died they wanted to take you on condition that I faded out of the picture. Well, I wasn't about to allow that to happen. It's a father's right to bring up his daughter, and thank God I've been able to do that without calling on their charity."

"So you come alone to balls?" Simon Adair said.

"Indeed, no." Her small hand stiffened on his arm and her chin jutted skywards. "Thomas drove me here in the carriage and will call for me promptly at eleven. Tizzie is most particular about my not staying out too late."

"I was not implying negligence," he said. "Who are your orphans?"

She gave him a startled glance, wondering when his questions would run out.

"You were feeding one," he reminded her.

"Oh, my father calls them orphans," she said, softening a little. "They may also be so."

"And?" He had paused as she seated herself on a bench.

"My besetting fault," she said quaintly, "is that I love

talking to people and I often find myself talking to other people whom—well, whom well-bred young ladies don't often meet, though I assure you they are perfectly respectable in their own sphere. There was the man who used to sweep the crossing. He was there every day in all weathers but nobody saw him—oh, they must have seen him but they never noticed him. I found myself talking to him one day and he was a French gentleman, an *émigré* who had fled from the Terror and had once ridden in his own carriage. Now don't you think that was a strange twist of fate? And there are so many children in the city, doing work that is far too heavy for them and very badly paid."

"You are a reformer," he accused, laughing.

"Oh, I hope not," she protested. "My father says that reformers have a bad habit of helping old ladies across the road when they don't want to cross."

"And your young friend with the beef patty?"

"He's a mudlark. You know, he sleeps under the arches of the bridge and looks at low tide for things he can sell. I met him when I went for a trip down the river one day. The guide on the boat was telling us all about Mr. Shakespeare and the Globe Theatre and I could only see those ragged boys fishing in the mud. Anyway when I come out to supper and a dance one of them usually hangs about waiting for a titbit."

"Some of those 'orphans' can be as tricky as monkeys," he warned. "Take care they are not looking out for unguarded doors while you're filching them a bite of supper."

"You clearly believe the worst of everybody," she said. "Is that why you carry a pistol?"

"How did—?" He looked down at her, startled.

"My father was a prizefighting manager at one time, and frequently carried a pistol because of the rough company he might encounter. It made a slight bulge under his arm."

"You have sharp eyes, Miss Sparrow." There was grudging admiration in his voice.

"And of course it is none of my business." She rose. "I really ought to go in now."

"Are you afraid of the pistol or of being compromised?" he enquired.

"Of neither," she said simply, "but Henry will be looking for me."

"You and Henry being—?"

"More or less. There is nothing definite yet, but he has intimated. It will be a good match for me."

"Now you have disappointed me," Simon Adair said. "I never thought you would marry for worldly reasons."

"I am not," she said tartly, "but it is congenial when both families approve of the union."

"Sir William and Lady Fairfax have been informed then?"

"Not exactly." She hesitated slightly. "Henry thinks that no girl should wed until she is twenty-one and fully adult and I am only just twenty. In a few weeks Henry means to speak to my father—and Lady Fairfax is always very civil to me."

"How did you and Henry meet?"

"Six months since." Her tone was light again. "I was walking in the park and it began to rain. Henry was kind enough to offer me shelter in his carriage and there we discovered that I had attended school with his cousin, and after that he called upon me and now I am invited to many of the functions at his home."

"He doesn't know about your crossing sweepers, mudlarks, and orphans?"

"He would think it most eccentric in me," she confessed. "He is, of course, very generous when it comes to various charities, and after we are married I hope to interest him in some of my more deserving cases—or less deserving. I never bother to distinguish between the two."

"Are you also hoping that the sun will rise in the west?" he asked bluntly.

"Meaning?" She had withdrawn her hand from his arm.

"Meaning that no Fairfax ever threw anything but a bucket of dirty water out of any window under which a member of the poor—deserving or otherwise—happened to be standing."

"That was an insufferable remark to make about your host, sir!"

"Fairfax would probably regard it as a compliment to his good sense," Simon Adair said. They were at the top of the steps again and she flung him an angry glance before she went ahead of him into the ballroom.

"There you are!" Henry hurried up, looking flustered. "Your coachman is below. Your father has had a serious accident."

The colour had fled from her face and she clutched at Henry.

"The physician has been called and Mrs. O'Hara has sent the coachman to fetch you home. I don't know any more than the—"

Before he had finished, Sparrow picked up her skirts and ran down the side of the room into the corridor beyond.

"What a delicate way you have of breaking bad news," Simon said dryly and strode after her. In the hall she was anxiously questioning a burly, red-faced coachman who towered over her slight figure. The questioning had turned to scolding by the time Simon reached the pair.

"How could you do anything so foolish? You know that Sultan is vicious and will not bear a rider."

"Wasn't my fault, Miss Sparrow," Thomas was protesting. "You know what your pa's like when he gets a notion in his head."

"How serious was the accident?" Simon stepped forward to ask.

"The physician hadn't arrived when Thomas left to collect me. Thank you, Sarah." She took her cloak from the maidservant.

"He was swearing something chronic," Thomas said gloomily.

"My father?" Sparrow's face brightened. "Then he has not suffered any head injury? It may not be quite as bad as I feared."

"Sure to be all right," Henry said, joining them. "I'd come back with you, but the other guests—"

12

"I'm riding back with Miss Harvey," Simon interrupted. "Will you have my horse saddled?"

"I'll see to it at once. Very good of you, Adair." Henry sounded grateful as he hurried away again.

"I have no need of escort," Sparrow began haughtily.

"I'll ride after the coach," Simon said firmly.

"Such an unfortunate accident." Lady Fairfax sailed towards them. "You will let us know if there is anything we can do?"

"Yes, of course. Thank you for inviting me, Lady Fairfax." Bobbing a hasty curtsey, Sparrow went out, holding the coachman's arm.

The Harvey home lay almost a mile from the Fairfax residence in a crescent almost equally imposing, though the buildings, seen close to, were smaller and shabbier. She had not always lived here. During her childhood Sparrow had known a variety of homes: lodgings occupied for varying periods, a delightful year when they had dwelt in a cottage in Chelsea, some tedious years at the Marylebone Academy for Young Ladies, and finally, for the last six years, this fine, tastefully furnished house.

"Nothing but the best for my girl!" Justin had cried, spreading wide his arms.

"You said that last time if I recall," Tizzie had said.

"Take no notice of the woman," Justin had advised, winking at Sparrow. "She's not accustomed to civilised living yet. In a month she'll be queening it over the neighborhood."

He was always optimistic and, in the six years since, it looked as if his optimism was justified. The various enterprises in which he was engaged began to yield a profit, and there was never any need to avoid the tradespeople who delivered their goods for lack of cash with which to pay the bills. She could not imagine what she would do if anything happened to her great-hearted father.

Tizzie, a shawl about her shoulders, was at the open door as the coach stopped. Sparrow scrambled out and ran up the steps, vaguely conscious that Simon Adair had tethered his horse to the railings and was following.

13

"Is it very bad, Tizzie?" She went past the older woman into the hall.

"The doctor just arrived," Tizzie said. "He suspects it's a broken left leg. Who's this?"

"Simon Adair. He followed me," Sparrow said, making for the stairs. Over her shoulder she added, "No need to fret. We know each other."

"I didn't imagine that you allowed complete strangers to follow you home," Tizzie said.

"I came as deputy for Mr. Henry Fairfax," Simon said, entering and sweeping Tizzie a bow, his vivid eyes on her plump frame, pretty face, and unexpected silvery grey hair.

"Did you indeed?" Tizzie said. "For my part I prefer a man who arrives on his own account."

"Mrs. O'Hara?"

"Well, at least Sparrow mentioned me," she said, somewhat mollified. "Come into the parlour. I'm in such a dither with the silly man trying to ride Sultan—whose last owner must have been the devil himself—and then the beast rearing, and bucking, and trampling the poor man."

"Where is the horse now?" Simon asked.

"Thomas and Ned—that's the bootboy—contrived to get him back in his stall."

"The horse is a recent purchase, I take it?"

"And no blame to the man who sold him," she said fairly. "He warned the master the great brute had never been ridden. After that nothing would suit him but he must buy it. Then he declared he'd be riding it by the time Sparrow came home from the ball. Was she much admired?"

"The cynosure of all eyes," Simon said.

"I knew it! That child could marry a prince, though she's so much like an aristocrat herself that I'd fear inbreeding." Tizzie looked triumphant. "Well, look at the poor king, God love him. Mad as a hatter! Is it true there's a permanent Regency set up now?"

"Quite true, Mrs. O'Hara."

"And Prinny sending Mrs. Fitzherbert away after all her

love and loyalty. Ingratitude, I call it! That sounds like the doctor calling, excuse me."

She bustled out, leaving him to wait. He spent the brief period in looking out of the door to check on the empty hall, then making a swift survey of the pleasant apartment, lifting a yellow-backed novel that lay open on the table, and running his fingers through a box of silks on one of the chairs. When Sparrow entered he was standing by the door.

"It is a broken leg," she said. She was still wearing her cloak, and against the black velvet her small face looked white and wan.

"Is there anything I can do?" Simon asked.

"Thank you, no. The bone has been splinted, and Thomas has helped to make him more comfortable. I am sorry not to be able to introduce you but he has just taken a strong dose of laudanum."

"You look as if you could do with some restorative yourself," he said.

"I believe there is some negus somewhere." She looked round vaguely, then bit her lip. "I do beg your pardon. I am completely forgetting my manners. May I offer you something?"

"Nothing, thank you. You must allow me to pour something for you."

"In the cabinet. It isn't locked." She spoke wearily, sinking into a chair as if her legs would no longer support her.

The carved cabinet in the corner held an array of bottles and decanters. He took out one of brandy and poured her a small measure.

"Thank you." Sparrow took a mouthful, shuddered, and sat upright as the colour flooded back into her cheeks. "It was rather a shock to hear—and poor Henry was so shocked himself that he was not as tactful as he might have been in telling me. He is excessively fond of Papa."

"I suppose that was why he rushed here and spoiled his pleasant evening," Simon said.

"He had social obligations," she said, jerking her chin at him angrily. "It was very kind of you to come back here with me, but Henry would certainly have offered had you not leapt in and signified your own intention. You know, if you go through the world attributing bad motives to every-body you meet, you must have a very undesirable frame of mind."

"I wasn't attributing any motives to Henry at all," Simon said blandly. "I think he acted according to his nature."

"If you will excuse me, Mr. Adair." She rose somewhat unsteadily, still clutching her brandy goblet. "I am going upstairs to sit with my father for a while. I'll ring for Susan to show you out."

"If you're hinting that I am not altogether welcome," he returned with his impish grin that made his harsh features more boyish, "you are not being very subtle."

"Good-night, sir." She took a step and tugged the edge of her cloak free from the arm of the chair.

"For someone who only took a mouthful of brandy you're somewhat unsteady on your feet," he commented.

"My father's accident has unnerved me," Sparrow said crossly. "Good-night."

"You also had a glass of wine with your supper. Shall I offer you my arm?"

"You are teasing me, Mr. Adair. I am merely very tired. Good-night." Her voice quavered slightly and she went out swiftly, her head bent. By the time she had mounted the stairs there were tears on her cheeks.

"Oh, Miss Sparrow, ain't it dreadful?" The maid of all work met her on the upper landing with a face full of excited gloom.

"A broken leg soon mends," Sparrow said. "There is a gentleman in the parlour. Please show him out."

"Is it Mr. Fairfax?" Susan asked as she went.

"Another gentleman."

But it ought to have been Henry who had brought her home, she thought, going softly into her father's room. It was a great pity that social obligations sometimes pre-vented him from acting with that generosity of spirit she was certain he possessed. She hoped she wouldn't have to meet Simon Adair again with his sarcastic tongue and brilliantly blue eyes. The kind of man who got sent down from the University and arrived uninvited at balls with a pistol tucked under his arm was not suitable company for any young lady's social list.

Her father was fast asleep and snoring slightly. Tizzie sat at the foot of the bed with a blanket round her.

Sparrow paused to listen to her father's snores, then tucked the blanket more tightly round Tizzie and went into her own bedroom, where she crossed to open the window, hoping to clear her head of its light dizziness.

In the sky, clusters of stars surrounded a moon as narrow as a leper's squint. She leaned her head against the window frame, closing her eyes, listening to the chimes of a distant clock.

Below her, Simon Adair moved back into the shadows. When the window above was closed again he trod silently to the gate, mounted his horse, took one last sweeping survey of the facade of the house, and rode away.

= 2 =

IN THE MORNING the world looked brighter. Sparrow, who had inherited her father's optimism, was cheered further when she put her head in at his door to see that he was still sleeping.

"And with luck he'll not start making a nuisance of himself until noon," Tizzie said when they sat down to breakfast. "That was a looker you brought home last night."

"I didn't bring him. He just followed me."

"I used to have the same trouble myself," Tizzie said reflectively. "I always thought it was a mercy that I wed the captain when I was so young, else I might have been tempted and fallen."

"Into what, Tizzie?" Sparrow asked, straight-faced.

"Into sin, shame, and pleasure, darling." Tizzie's pretty face crinkled into laughter. "As it was, the captain fell fathoms deep in love the first time of laying eyes on me and before I knew it I was trotting up the aisle. That was a wonderful year we had. It was a tragedy that he went so young. One unlucky blow when he let his guard down, and there I was a widow. If it hadn't been for your father, God love him, I'd have been lost."

Justin Harvey had offered her the post of nurse to his baby daughter, saying, "I was the captain's manager, Tizzie, and he'd not thank me for leaving his wife to fend for herself. You'll be taking potluck with us, my dear, but I've a feeling that Sparrow will be safe in your hands."

"We'd both have been lost without you, Tizzie," Sparrow said now with affection. "You stuck with us through the bad times."

"Yes, well, as to that," Tizzie hesitated, crumbling bread on her plate, shaping it into tiny molehills.

"It is only a broken leg, isn't it?" Sparrow spoke sharply. "You are not hiding some evil news from me, are you?"

"Bless your heart, why would I be doing that?" Tizzie exclaimed, blushing. "No, a broken leg is all it is that's wrong. The physician told me it will likely heal as good as new. Strong as a bull your father is, thank the Lord."

"Then what is bothering you?" Sparrow, who could read every nuance in the expressions that flitted across the older woman's face, frowned at her.

"Ups and downs," Tizzie said. "Did all the gentlemen really admire you last evening?"

"What ups and downs?"

"A little temporary difficulty in the financial sphere," Tizzie said.

"How temporary?"

"A matter of cash flow," Tizzie said. "Your father was hoping to recoup his losses but with himself laid up it may prove a problem."

"Surely we've plenty to tide us over until he's on his feet again?"

"The trouble is that the bills won't wait any longer," Tizzie said.

"What bills? Father's been doing so well these past few years."

"He's been on a winning streak," the other admitted, "but it's turning sour again. The shares he bought in that West Indian sugar plantation, for example."

"That was an excellent investment."

"Yes, it was, but the slaves on the plantation revolted and destroyed the crops."

"What?" Sparrow's face had paled. "When did you hear this?"

"A couple of months back."

"A couple of months," Sparrow echoed. "Why didn't you tell me?"

"We were hoping the situation would improve," Tizzie

said sadly. "Not that it won't—in time, but time's what we haven't got. There's the rent due."

"Rent for what?" Sparrow asked in bewilderment, seeing that Tizzie had broken off short.

"Nothing for you to bother your head about. I'm just running on because your father's being thrown gave me such a turn. More coffee?"

"Rent for what, Tizzie?" A small hand reached and fastened on the housekeeper's wrist.

"The house," Tizzie said reluctantly.

"This house? Why should we pay rent on our own property?"

"It isn't exactly our own," Tizzie confessed. "Your father rented it. He wanted you to have a good address now that you're growing up, starting to go out and about in Society."

"He didn't buy it?" Sparrow drew a long breath, trying to come to terms with the revelation.

"Well, surely we can find the rent? We can sell something. Those vases in the drawing-room—"

"We rented the place furnished," Tizzie said.

"You mean none of this belongs to us? Not any of it?"

"Only a few bits and pieces we brought from the last place," Tizzie said. "I shouldn't have told you. Your father will half kill me if he ever finds out that you know. You were due back from school, you see, and things were looking up for us. He wanted you to have a nice place."

"So I could make my social debut," Sparrow said bitterly.

"And it would all have gone right," Tizzie said, "if those slaves hadn't burned the crops and your father hadn't broken his leg. How can he recoup his losses when he's laid up?"

"My jewellery is mine," Sparrow said. "Isn't it?"

"You can't sell that," Tizzie said with decision. "The pearls belonged to your poor mama, and the watch and bracelets were bought with your father's first winnings after he buried her. And they wouldn't fetch much anyway."

"The new horse? Sultan?"

"Bought the nasty creature cheap and it won't be easy to sell him off again."

"Perhaps we had better go through the accounts?" Sparrow suggested.

"Oh, I couldn't let you do that, dear." Tizzie looked shocked. "Your father never wanted you to be bothered with finances. He's of the opinion that young ladies should go to balls and parties and not trouble about the little annoyances of life."

"We won't tell him," Sparrow said grimly. "Bring the account books, Tizzie, and whatever else you can find in his desk."

Tizzie opened her mouth to argue, closed it again, and rose reluctantly.

"We'll go through them in the parlour so that Susan can clear away." Sparrow also rose, telling herself firmly that matters couldn't possibly be as bad as Tizzie was hinting.

Half an hour later she raised her head from the accounts, added up a final sum on her fingertips, and presented an appalled face to her companion who sat opposite.

"We appear," she said, "to be on the verge of ruin."

"Over the verge," Tizzie corrected.

"There is one hundred pounds' rent to be found and the tradesmen to pay."

"Trifling sums." Tizzie looked uncomfortable.

"It comes to one hundred and fifty pounds plus the dressmaker to be paid. I would not have ordered all those new gowns had I known. Who owns the house?"

"Some old gentleman who lives abroad. We pay the rent to a firm of solicitors."

"The ones who wrote this letter reminding Father that the rent is overdue?"

Tizzie nodded, looking miserable.

"I've been thinking of getting a job," she said. "I used to work in my uncle's tavern before I met the captain."

"Tizzie, you couldn't possibly. You know you would hate it," Sparrow said. "And what would Father do without you? Or me? We have neither of us the least notion how to get on without you."

"That's very sweet of you, dearie, and I appreciate it," Tizzie said warmly, "but it isn't solving the problem."

"There is my dowry. Perhaps I can raise a loan on the promise of—no dowry?"

"Two hundred pounds," Tizzie said.

"Two hundred? But there used to be fifteen hundred. What happened to it? No, don't bother to tell me. I can guess." The grey eyes were stormy. "He speculated with it in an attempt to increase it instead of leaving it at interest somewhere safe and reliable."

"I don't care to hear what sounds like a criticism of your father," Tizzie reproved.

"I'm not criticising him," Sparrow cried. "He's having another run of bad luck, I know, but some of it is surely due to his own lack of thought. How could he have left me sitting in a fool's paradise? How could you?"

Tizzie burst into tears, her plump shoulders heaving.

"Oh, please don't cry," Sparrow begged. "I know that you both acted for the best, in my interests, but the fact remains that nothing is exactly as I had thought. And we cannot worry Father with it at this time. So we must put our heads together and contrive to get out of the mess."

"How?" Tizzie asked, blowing her nose.

"We can pay the rent and the immediate bills from the dowry—"

"But that's for your marriage. You cannot go through the world without a dowry."

"Don't make such a drama out of it," Sparrow said, feeling herself become calmer as the other became more agitated. "If any man offers for me simply because of my dowry then he is not worth the having. Now that is only a short-term solution."

"But that is all that's required," Tizzie said. "Henry Fairfax will be talking to his parents and to your father soon, and by then your father will be on his feet again and able to get your dowry up to scratch."

"We had best keep this from him until he is feeling

better," Sparrow said. "And I do think it would be a good idea to retrench a little. The bills for meat are very high."

"Your father will only eat the best cuts," Tizzie mourned.

"Then the rest of us must make do with the rest of the animal," Sparrow said firmly. "Put these back now. You have authority to draw upon the bank, haven't you? Then go and rescue the remainder of my dowry and put the last fifty pounds somewhere safe where Father cannot speculate with it. And don't begin to cry again or he will imagine that he is suffering from some terrible disease."

"I only hope that you can bring Henry Fairfax up to the mark very soon" was Tizzie's parting remark.

Henry had plenty of money, Sparrow reflected, and wouldn't give a hang if she had no dowry at all. She hoped her estimation of his character was right and then scolded herself for doubting.

By midday her father was awake and demanding sustenance. Sparrow, putting her head in at his door, was greeted irritably.

"Rotten business this, hey, girl? That horse is a devil. Must be to throw me for I swear I can ride anything on four legs. I planned to race him at Newmarket but that's gone down the drain now. I shall sell him, and take the loss like a man. What possessed Tizzie to lose her head and send Thomas to drag you away from the ball? Was it a good one?"

"Very pleasant," Sparrow said cautiously. "Lady Fairfax asked after you."

"Very civil of her seeing she doesn't know me from Adam," he growled. "When am I going to meet Henry's parents?"

"When your leg is healed," Sparrow said. "You must take life very quietly for a week or two."

"Why? Are the Fairfaxes so exciting that they will give me a heart attack or something? Then they are very different from their son. That is a very dull young man you have caught for yourself. However, if it's what you want, you'd best reel him in. What do you want?"

23

The last query was flung at Tizzie, who entered with a bowl of soup and a timid smile.

"Nourishment," she said and cast a pleading glance towards Sparrow.

"That," said Justin Harvey, peering suspiciously into the depths of the bowl, "is pap, not nourishment. I'll have a couple of lamb chops and some eggs."

"And work your system into a fever? The physician will be furious with me for allowing it."

"You don't have the authority to allow or forbid anything," he retorted. "You're employed as housekeeper."

"And you couldn't manage without her," Sparrow said, "so drink your soup."

"You, my dear girl, are becoming a strong-minded woman," he said gloomily. "I fear the day is dawning when I can no longer bully you."

"You never did," Sparrow said, blowing him a kiss as she went out. Her smile faded as she went down the stairs. Tizzie's revelations had shocked her out of the security in which she fancied she had been living. Her universe was suddenly based on sand, with a house and furniture that didn't belong to them, a dowry that seemed to have melted away, and bills that would continue to come in even after the present ones had been settled. Henry would have to make a definite offer very soon. Then she would be off her father's hands and he would no longer feel compelled to live above his means.

The clip-clop of hooves in the streets announced Henry. Glimpsing him from the window, she hurried to the front door.

"Was the accident very severe?" he enquired, dismounting and tethering his horse to the railings.

"A broken leg, as Thomas suspected," she said. "Perhaps it would be better if we walked out in the park. My father is not in a good humour."

"I'll wait," he said, relief on his face.

Grabbing her pelisse from behind the door, she wished

that Henry and her father were more compatible, but the most they had achieved was a kind of neutral courtesy.

"I thought you would have come by earlier," she began, having joined him outside.

"Overslept," Henry said. "The ball went on until four and I was worn out."

"Oh." Her voice was small and flat.

"Not that I'd be of any use in a sickroom," he continued. "Never sure what to say to cheer invalids up. Anyway, I'm here on a different matter."

"Oh?" She looked up at him as they crossed the road and began to stroll along the riverbank.

"You and I have been very close, wouldn't you say?"

"I thought we were." Her heart had begun to beat uncomfortably fast.

"We get along well," Henry said. "Not that Mother altogether approves. Oh, she likes you well enough. It isn't that."

"What isn't that?" she asked carefully.

"Matter of what they expect of me actually," Henry said. "My father's hoping to be created a peer as soon as the Regency gets into its stride. That's very often a matter of whom you know rather than what you do. Well, the point is that—he would be very happy if I paid more attention to Jane Marquis. I won't, of course. Heavens above, a man has to choose his own wife; can't rely on this father to pick one out even for the sake of a peerage, but I'm treading warily. No sense in upsetting them."

Jane Marquis had dark smooth hair and lisped slightly. She was very well bred and had probably never heard of mudlarks, let alone fed one.

"We are not officially engaged," Sparrow said. "You are under no obligation. In fact, you would do better to forget any notion of wedding me since my dowry is very small and my social influence nil."

"Lord, I wouldn't dream of trying to get out of anything." Henry looked upset. "And if your dowry is very small than I'd certainly do the honourable thing. No question."

Now was the moment when any girl of sense would urge him to marry her at once and present his parents with a *fait accompli*. Sparrow could only conclude that she had no sense at all as she heard herself say calmly, "I am really relieved that you should be feeling this way, Henry dear, because I've been trying to think of a way of letting you down lightly. The friendship we have for each other isn't sufficient for matrimony, especially in the face of your parents' disapproval."

"If you genuinely feel like that—?"

"Oh, I do, Henry. I genuinely do," she assured him.

In all the novels she and Tizzie read, this was the signal for the hero to sweep her into his arms and declare that he loved her passionately and would, if necessary, hold her captive until she agreed to be his wife.

The novels were no indication of the course real life took. Henry's fair skin had reddened but there was relief at the back of his eyes.

"We must always be devoted friends," he said, pressing her hands warmly.

"Yes indeed," she said mechanically.

"And Mama would be devastated if you no longer came to see us."

Sparrow felt like saying that Lady Fairfax was unlikely to be completely devastated, but she heroically held her tongue.

"If there is ever anything I can do?" He had released her hand and looked as if he were about to break into a dance.

She was tempted to enquire how he felt about lending her a large sum of money at minimum interest, but merely murmured, "I must get back to my father. Do thank your mother for her concern."

It was fortunate they had not walked very far. A few minutes brought them back to the house, where Henry mounted his horse, assured her once more of his undying loyalty, and rode off, a trifle too jauntily to be taken as a man disappointed in love.

"Missy Sparrow, someone wants to buy that animal that threw Mr. Harvey," Thomas announced, emerging from the entry at the side of the house as she was about to let herself in.

"Why, that's marvellous." Her downcast face brightened. "Let us go and clinch the sale at once, before Sultan reveals his true nature. I did not realise that Father had advertised—oh, it's you."

She had hurried down the entry into the stable yard and stopped short, her voice fading away as Simon Adair strolled towards her.

"Good day, Miss Sparrow. I am delighted to learn from Thomas that your father is recovering," he said amiably.

It was the first time she had seen him in daylight, and she was startled at the effect he had on her. He was browner of skin than most fashionable young gentlemen, and his hair was of that particular shade of brunette that has a blue sheen in sunlight. Despite his formal manner and correct attire, there was something dangerously gypsylike about him.

"You have forgotten me," he said sadly. "Alas, it is my fate not to leave a permanent mark upon the memories of those with whom I wish to seek further acquaintance. Perhaps if I were to wade into the shallows of the river and start—"

"What can I do for you, Mr. Adair?" she broke in hastily. "Thomas said that someone wished to buy Sultan, but—"

"Provided the animal is for sale, Miss Sparrow. I like a spirited mount."

"This one is unrideable, sir. My father is an experienced horseman but even he was thrown as you already know."

"Oh, I daresay I shall contrive to keep my seat," he said with an indifferent air. "Is he perpetually vicious?"

"He is a lamb until someone tries to sit on him. I warned Father—"

"Perhaps we could have him out here. No saddle. A halter will suffice."

"Lead Sultan out, Thomas," Sparrow said. "Mr. Adair, you really must think again before you attempt to ride him. I cannot be responsible for the consequences if you try."

"I will take the responsibility," he said, beginning to strip off his coat and loosen the cravat at his neck.

Sparrow cast her eyes up to the small patch of sky visible beyond the high walls of yard and alley and hastily skipped aside as Thomas led the black stallion out of the stall.

"He truly is a sultan," Simon breathed. "Proud as Arabia, aren't you, my lad?" He was walking slowly forwards, both hands held palms outward. The vivid blue eyes were fixed on the horse. Thomas had dropped the reins and stood back against the wall.

"Sultan? Sultan, my lovely boy. My proud beauty. You are not sure yet, but you have just met your master. We'll ride together, you and I, to the edge of the world if that's my fancy. *Kushti*, Sultan. *Dordi grai. Hele, hele.*"

The words he spoke were strange to her, singing into the air. His voice caressed, teased, and invited. Under the thin lawn of his shirt his shoulders were wide, curls of black hair sprang above the loosened cravat, his thighs were long muscled in the cream buckskins that encased them.

The stallion stood stock-still, only the ears pricked. One foreleg pawed the cobbles.

"*Dordi* Sultan," the voice caressed, each syllable stroking the heart. Simon blew softly into the quivering nostrils only inches from his own harsh, dark features.

"We'll make music together," he said and leapt, light as wind, to the broad back. There was a space between heartbeat and heartbeat, and then the great stallion reared, the man on its back clinging close, the voice rising to a crooning note that held an undercurrent of excitement.

"You and I, *kushti* Sultan. *Hele, hele.*"

Hooves struck the cobbles with a high ringing sound, and then both rider and mount were galloping down the entry, the man's triumphant laughter mingling with the beating of the hooves.

"He'll break his neck," William gasped, rushing into the entry.

"He will not," Sparrow said. "Not him."

She felt as if she had been held in the grip of a dream, gentled like the stallion. Slowly she moved down the entry and stood by Thomas, watching the pair jump the wall that led to the riverbank and thunder over the turf, the gleaming white shirt one note of brightness in the black.

"That gentleman is a positive centurion," Thomas said solemnly. "I never saw anything to beat it."

"I think you mean centaur, Thomas," Sparrow said, "but you are absolutely right."

"You ought to have made a wager with me, Miss Sparrow," Simon called, trotting back at a more decorous pace.

"I never gamble, Mr. Adair," she said primly. "Oh, but that was truly magnificent. Where did you learn to ride like that?"

"My great-grandmother was a Boswell," he informed her, sliding to the ground, handing the rein to Thomas, "A Romany. Horses are in the blood. Horses and beautiful women and the desire for conquest."

"Was that Romany? The words you spoke?"

"They convey meaning better than solemn English." They were walking back together into the yard and he bent to pick up his coat. "I will give you fifty guineas for him. He is worth more but I cannot afford more, and I doubt that many would be able to ride him."

"Father certainly couldn't. Fifty guineas sounds a very fair price. I shall have to consult my father first since the horse belongs to him." She spoke in brisk, clipped tones, striving to regain her equilibrium. It would never do to allow Mr. Simon Adair to realise that he had stirred something within her that was primitive and exciting and most unladylike.

"Naturally," he agreed. "On the other hand, your father might be relieved of the necessity of having to argue about the matter if it were a foregone conclusion."

"You must have met him already."

"Only by hearsay. He is known as a gentleman who sticks to his own opinions but relishes being argued out of them."

"That's Father," she agreed. "Oh, won't you come in? I must ask Tizzie where the original bill of sale is so that transfer of ownership can be recorded."

She had opened the side door and was leading the way past the kitchen to the stairs. "I hope you don't object to a back door? I often use it myself." She threw him a questioning glance as they mounted to the hall.

"I frequently use back doors myself," he assured her. "Saves scandal, doesn't it?"

"You would know more than I do about such matters surely, Mr. Adair?"

"*Touché*, Miss Sparrow."

He showed his blunt white teeth in an appreciative grin as they went into the parlour.

"Tizzie will be down in a moment. She will know where the bill of sale is." Sparrow removed her pelisse and smoothed down her gown, determined to be cool and collected.

"Was that Henry's horse outside when I arrived?" he asked.

"He and I were taking a short walk. Your own horse is—"

"A friend of mine gave me a ride here and will call back in a little while. Was Henry proposing to you?"

"I fail to see what concern of yours—" She caught his eye and said with resignation, "He was trying to wriggle out of proposing to me. I helped him to contrive it with the least embarrassment."

"I was rather afraid of that." He eyed her for a moment, then said, "Miss Marquis is an excellent catch."

"And I am not—no, you need not disclaim the thought. I can read your mind."

"Oh, I do hope not," he exclaimed. "At this moment I cannot decide whether the desire to knock Henry out or kiss you is uppermost in my mind."

"I would prefer you did neither," she said hastily. "Henry has every right to wed where he wishes, and the first man whose kisses I invite must come with a proposal of marriage."

"Then I will have to forgo both desires," he said sadly, "since I cannot fight a man who has not offended you and I have no intention of marrying until I am at least forty and in need of a permanent housekeeper."

"I had not issued any invitation," she said darkly.

"Had you not?" His blue eyes travelled over her face as if he were touching her flesh with his gaze.

"I do wonder where Tizzie is," she said, moving to the door.

"Probably resting, if she has been up all night tending the invalid. I will send my man round later on with the money and he can sign for the horse. Is it true that your father has suffered financial reverses recently?"

"Who told you?" she asked blankly.

"There was some talk at White's this morning. Several gentlemen have lost heavily because of the trouble on the plantations. For some it is no more than a temporary hiccough. I suspect it is rather more than that for Mr. Harvey."

"We are in a difficult situation" she admitted. "It is not something I can discuss with my father since he doesn't believe females should be involved in business problems."

"In my experience most business problems are caused by females, so why shouldn't they help to solve them? A definite proposal from Henry Fairfax would have been useful, I gather?"

"It would have got me off Father's hands," she sighed, "but the truth is that Henry was never truly in love with me nor I with him. So my conduct was not in the least noble."

"Miss Sparrow," he returned gravely, "in the course of what I hope will be a long and mutual friendship I may accuse you of many things, but I don't think that nobility will be among them."

"I am as likely to accuse you of gallantry," she flashed.

"I am not often guilty of that either," he agreed. "So what do you intend to do? Find a rich husband? Rich husbands generally marry rich wives and become more prosperous."

"I really don't see why you should concern yourself with my future," she said crossly.

"Neither do I," he said, "but it seems to be another bad habit I am adding to my catalogue of vices. What will you do?"

"I haven't the faintest idea," she confessed. "What can I possibly do?"

"You might try working," he suggested.

"Working? For my living?" Sparrow gaped at him. "I wasn't brought up to it."

"I can see that." He gave her a faintly disdainful glance. "You were brought up to be useless and charming and a potential problem for any luckless gentleman who hasn't got a bottomless purse. Oh, you salve your conscience by handing out titbits to ragged urchins. That satisfies your sense of adventure, no doubt. But the idea of actually finding a position and earning money at it never entered your head."

"But what could I possibly do?" She was too astonished to be angry. "You are not saying that I should go into service, I trust?"

"You would probably make a dreadful parlour-maid," he agreed. "Governess? Dressmaker?"

"I hate sewing."

"Do you hate children too?"

"No, I like most children, I think." She looked at him doubtfully. "Oh, but Father would never countenance such a notion."

"A tyrant, is he?" Simon said.

"No, of course not." The image of her father's handsome, slightly dissipated features rose in her mind. "He has a quick temper with no bite behind it," she said at last, "but he has a great deal of pride. I cannot take that from him by applying for a position—even a temporary one."

"Then it will have to be the rich husband since you cannot think of a way round your dilemma. Ah, there is my friend. My man will be round later. That stallion and I will get along splendidly together. He rises to a challenge."

He sketched a salute and was gone, leaving her to watch as he ran lightly down the front steps and climbed up into a curricle.

The driver of the curricle relinquished the reins and moved over onto the passenger seat. Sparrow got a glimpse of high-piled black hair and a Grecian profile under a dashing hat trimmed with scarlet feathers before the vehicle bowled away again.

"Well," Sparrow said indignantly. "Well indeed."

"Well indeed what? And who just went out?" Tizzie demanded, coming in.

"I sold Sultan to Mr. Adair for fifty guineas so we can pay the dressmaker as well as everybody else. His man is coming round later for the bill of sale. Do you think Father will agree?"

"You leave your father to me, dear," Tizzie asserted.

"You haven't told him that I am aware of the situation?"

"Lord, no. I don't want ructions," Tizzie said. "I'm just praying that Henry Fairfax asks—"

"I have released Henry from any sense of obligation towards me," Sparrow said formally.

"You *never* have?" Tizzie sat down heavily. "You were in love with him."

"Not in a *kushti* kind of way."

"In a what?"

"Never mind. Tizzie, what would you do if I told you that I was going to apply for a post as a governess?"

"Faint dead away," Tizzie said firmly.

"Nonsense, you cannot possibly faint while you are sitting down," Sparrow said. "Oh, I do not intend to become a governess for ever. That would be quite dreadful, I imagine, not least for the poor pupils. But Father will be laid up for six or seven weeks and we will require money. I see no point in running up more debts."

"He will never agree," Tizzie warned.

"We won't tell him," Sparrow said. "I shall accept an invitation from an old school friend to visit her for a month."

"Governesses are expected to stay for longer than a month," Tizzie said.

"There must be occasions when a governess has to be replaced for a short time, if she is ill or something," Sparrow said. "I wonder where one would apply."

"There's an agency, I believe," Tizzie said vaguely. "I can ask Thomas. Sparrow, are you sure this is necessary?"

"I need a challenge," Sparrow said, and repeated it as if she had just discovered the fact for herself. "I need a challenge, Tizzie."

═ 3 ═

SPARROW SMOOTHED DOWN her dress for the tenth time and glanced pointedly at the large clock in the corner. She had been waiting for nearly an hour in the outer office of the agency and in her opinion it was too long.

She had come with Thomas, who was now eating his dinner in the hostelry at the corner of the road while she sat, tapping her foot, and being studiously ignored by the balding clerk behind the high desk at the top of the dingy room.

"Hilton?" The clerk looked up as a bell clanged from the inner office. Sparrow jumped slightly, recognising the name she had given.

"Mrs. Carstairs will interview you now," the clerk said, looking unhappy at the prospect. Sparrow rose with deliberate dignity. Being patronised was not something to which she intended to become accustomed. The other ladies waiting with her shot looks of envy in her direction. It had crossed her mind that they were all clad far more shabbily than she was, though she had put on her plainest dress and bonnet.

The inner office was larger than the outer one, boasting a square of carpet and a flat-topped desk at which a mannish-looking woman, severe in black and white, was seated.

"Sarah Hilton?" Her voice was as crisp as her outfit.

Sparrow curtsied. She was not well known in Society but Sparrow had sounded too distinctive a name for a potential governess.

35

"Sit down." Mrs. Carstairs indicated a small, hard chair placed where the light from the window at the side fell full on the face of the occupant.

Sparrow sat down, folded her hands in her lap, and fixed large grey eyes on the other.

"Age?" The word was snapped out.

"Twenty-two," Sparrow said, unblushingly adding a couple of years.

"And you are seeking a post as a governess? What previous experience have you had?"

"This will be my first post."

There would have been no sense in lying about that since she might have been asked for some proof.

"You are rather old to be seeking a post for the first time," Mrs. Carstairs said.

"There have been family reverses." That was certainly true, she reflected.

"What subjects can you offer?"

"English, history, geography, and arithmetic. Music too," she added.

"Are you fluent in any foreign language?"

"French."

"You can, of course, offer needlework?"

Of all things she hated sewing, but as Tizzie said it was not necessary to enjoy something in order to teach it.

"Of course."

"You have two references? No, if this is your first post you will not. Nevertheless, a letter from your clergyman will be required. You are an Anglican?" The glance accompanying the question was so suspicious that Sparrow was almost tempted to claim she was a Moslem. She resisted the temptation and meekly nodded.

"You have younger brothers and sisters perhaps?"

"No, ma'am, but I like children," Sparrow assured her.

"It is not necessary for a governess to like children," the other said quellingly. "Only that she be capable of controlling them."

"I don't think that someone who dislikes children ought to be a governess at all," Sparrow argued. "I think that—"

"Miss Hilton, we are not here to learn what you think," Mrs. Carstairs said sharply. "Now the Goddens are looking for a nursery governess for their three youngest children."

"I couldn't take the post for more than six weeks," Sparrow said.

"Six weeks. You are looking then for temporary employment? You ought to have made that clear from the beginning. Six weeks is a very short period indeed."

"I thought I might stand in for someone who was sick or on holiday."

"My dear Miss Hilton, governesses do not take holidays." Mrs. Carstairs's voice had risen perceptibly.

"But they get sick, don't they? Break their legs and things?"

"I have not yet heard of any governess breaking her leg," Mrs. Carstairs said repressively.

"Maybe they shoot them," Sparrow said and choked back a giggle.

"A temporary position will be much more difficult to arrange. The Coxes are between governesses. Theirs died only three months before she was to be retired."

She made it sound as if the governess had died on purpose.

"That might suit me," Sparrow said.

"It is a question of whether you would suit them," her interviewer said severely. "They have twin daughters who are due to come out in six months' time so the post is more chaperone than teacher. They require someone for two months—at eight pounds."

"Only eight pounds?" Sparrow said.

"I fail to understand what you mean by 'only,' Miss Hilton," Mrs. Carstairs said. "That is a most generous salary. Most generous."

"I was hoping to make about fifty pounds," Sparrow said.

"Miss Hilton, I cannot imagine where you received your

own education." Mrs. Carstairs snapped shut the ledger in front of her. "No governess in the world could expect to earn more than fifty pounds a year and that would be a most experienced teacher who could offer a wide variety of subjects. Certainly a chit of a girl with no experience and, if I may say so, a most unbecoming levity of manner, could not hope to earn more than fifteen pounds per year, less laundry expenses. Now, if you will excuse me, I have other candidates to see." She jerked her head towards the door in a manner that admitted of no refusal. There was nothing for Sparrow to do but rise, make the obligatory curtsey, and withdraw with her head high.

She and Tizzie had never realised that governesses came so low in the scale of salaries. Eight pounds would do very little to solve the immediate financial problems. Outside in the street she breathed in the fresh air with pleasure. How dreadful it must be to sit hour after hour in that musty place waiting for a position that paid so little. Why a barmaid could probably earn more! She crossed the road thoughtfully and sat down on a circular bench enclosing a plane tree to consider the matter.

She had never been in a tavern in her life, and if she were contemplating such an act then she would have to deceive Tizzie as well as her father. It was too complicated. Perhaps she could get a job on the stage. She had an excellent memory and a clear voice—and not the faintest idea how to go about doing that either. It began to look as if Simon Adair had been right and she had been reared to be completely useless.

Probably the most sensible course of action would be to go and tell Thomas she was ready to go home and forget all the nonsense about earning money.

From the other side of the tree there came a soft, muffled sound. Sparrow was not so intent on her own problems that she failed to recognise weeping when she heard it. Rising and circling in the direction of the sound, she came upon a slender figure huddled disconsolately on the other half of the bench. The figure was female, with curly brown hair feathering a pale and woebegone countenance under a closed straw bonnet. As Sparrow cleared her throat the girl raised her eyes from a scrap of lacy handkerchief and gave a weak and wavering smile.

"I'm sorry if I disturbed you," she said apologetically. "I thought I was by myself."

"I can go away again if you like," Sparrow offered, but the girl put out a pleading hand.

"Oh, please don't leave on my account. I shall control myself the more easily if I have company. It is shockingly missish of me to behave like this," she said gulpingly.

"Perhaps it would help to talk about it?" Sparrow said, her ready sympathy roused by the other's evident distress.

"I wouldn't want to impose," the other said doubtfully.

"Oh, you wouldn't be imposing at all," Sparrow assured her. "I am feeling so miserable myself that to listen to someone else's troubles might cheer me up—oh dear, I didn't mean that in exactly the way it sounded."

"I'm sure you did not." The other girl gave a shaky little laugh. "I hope your own troubles are not overwhelming."

"I need to earn some money and I am just discovering that I am not very well qualified to do so," Sparrow said.

"You mean you are free to accept employment?"

"Eager would be a better word," Sparrow admitted. "I need a respectable position that lasts for about six weeks and pays more than governessing."

"Oh, but this seems like Fate." The girl sat up straight, all traces of tears gone, her eyes bright with sudden hope.

"Does it?" Sparrow wondered what she was talking about.

"If you can spare me a little time I can explain all," her new companion said. Thomas would have had his meal by now but, being under orders to wait, would linger over his ale.

"Yes?" Sparrow put on an encouraging expression.

"First I must tell you who I am," the girl said. "My name is Marie Sinclair."

"Sparrow Harvey. How do you do?"

"In great tribulation of mind, I'm afraid," Marie Sinclair said. "I have lost my fiancé."

"I'm most terribly sorry," Sparrow said in shocked sympathy.

"No, he is not deceased—at least I don't think he is, but I cannot be sure. I cannot be sure of anything, and it is tearing me to pieces."

"If you could explain?" Sparrow suggested.

"My fiancé's name is Adam Stuart," Marie said. "Our betrothal is private as yet. My uncle, with whom I make my home, is ambitious for a better match for me. He is inclined to disapprove of my feelings for Adam. However, Adam has very wealthy and respectable connections in Scotland, where his family originated. His great-uncle has always hinted that he intends to make Adam his heir, and so Adam travelled up to Scotland to stay with the old gentleman. He intended to inform him of the affection between us and obtain a definite promise about his eventual inheritance and then there will be far more likelihood of my uncle's consenting to our marriage. Adam is not a fortune hunter."

She placed particular emphasis upon the last phrase, which led Sparrow to suspect that the young lady's uncle had accused him of being one.

"You said you had lost him," she gently prompted.

"He went up to Scotland three months ago," Marie said, "and has neither written to me nor returned. Not one letter, though we swore solemnly to write every week."

"Perhaps your uncle confiscated the letters?" Sparrow suggested.

"I make a point of meeting the postman every morning as he approaches the house," Marie said.

"Then perhaps he was—" Sparrow hesitated, then plunged on. "Perhaps he was not as bound to you in affection as you imagined him to be? It is not a happy prospect to face, but it can sometimes happen. I have personal experience of that, unfortunately."

"If Adam had decided not to marry me, which is quite unthinkable, he would have returned to London and informed me personally. He has great moral courage," Marie said firmly.

"Would his own relative have informed you in the event of an accident?"

"I don't know." Marie produced the handkerchief again and dabbed her eyes. "Oh, surely he would, for though he was not aware of my existence, Adam was going to tell him as soon as he reached Craig Bothwell."

"Is that where his great-uncle lives?"

"It is the name of the family estate in the west of Scotland," Marie nodded.

"And you've heard nothing?"

"Not one word." The other shook her head. "He travelled up by stage and I made enquiries at the office but there have been no accidents."

"And you have written to him?"

"Every week," Marie said dismally, "but to no avail. He must have reached his destination, else my letters would surely have been returned. I am quite in despair, Miss Harvey."

"I don't see how I can be of help," Sparrow said, adding hastily, "though I would if it were possible, I do assure you."

"But it is possible," Marie said. "You said you were looking for temporary employment. It would be possible, would it not, for you to travel to Scotland to make some discreet enquiries? I am willing to pay you handsomely, for my uncle gives me a most generous allowance."

"But why cannot you go yourself?" Sparrow began, then checked herself. "Oh, I suppose your uncle would not allow it."

"The last time he saw Adam he ordered him from the house," Marie said miserably. "Adam tried to explain that he has considerable expectations, but my uncle simply refused to listen. He certainly would not countenance my going off to look for him. It is quite hard for me to slip away for long enough to walk in the park or down by the river. I am only here now because my maid had leave to visit her sister who lives in the vicinity."

41

"Why can't you send your maid to look for him?" Sparrow asked, wondering if she was arguing herself out of a situation which would vastly improve her financial condition.

"I do have some pride," Marie said. Faint colour stained her pale cheeks. "I cannot believe that Adam has deserted me, but how truly dreadful if the unthinkable had happened and I were to send someone known to him up to the estate. It would be a crushing humiliation."

"But I can hardly arrive unannounced and bang on the door demanding to know the whereabouts of Adam Stuart," Sparrow said sensibly."

"Perhaps you could be seeking a position there?" Marie gnawed her lower lip thoughtfully. "Craig Bothwell is somewhat remote. I recall Adam telling me once that they could not get servants to stay for very long."

"I really don't know—" Sparrow glanced down the road towards the tavern. Thomas would certainly emerge very soon to see if there was any sign of her.

"I suppose it would be a dreadful imposition," Marie said. Her voice was shaking again. "You have been very patient in the listening. It was only that you did mention you sought employment, and I thought a hundred guineas—"

Sparrow, in the act of rising, sat down again abruptly. "That is a considerable sum," she said slowly.

"And if you obtained a position that money would be extra," Marie said. "I would also pay your carriage fare up to Scotland."

"You want me to find Adam Stuart and tell him of your concern?"

"Only find him," Marie begged. "If he is unhurt then it is clear he has some other reason for not communicating with me, and I will not shame myself by demanding an explanation he has not yet volunteered. There is no need for him to learn of the connection between us."

"And I am to tell you if I find him? How?"

"If you wrote to me—Marie Sinclair, Number Eight, Beaumont Gardens," the other said. "It would be for me to decide what to do then. Oh, but I have only fifty guineas on me."

"Only?" Sparrow echoed.

"I could leave the other fifty at the stagecoach office in Marylebone with your ticket," Marie said eagerly. "The stage goes twice a week via York and Carlisle. Oh, I cannot tell you how grateful—"

"But how do you know you can trust me?" Sparrow demanded. "I might take the money and vanish as thoroughly as Adam has done."

"I cannot believe that when an answer to prayer comes it would end in such treachery," Marie said. "You will not vanish, will you?"

"No, of course not. It is only that—Scotland seems a very long way off," Sparrow said.

"But would it not be a challenge for a lady seeking employment?" Marie questioned.

That wretched word again, as if her whole life had been spent in avoiding risk.

"It would certainly solve my immediate problems," Sparrow admitted, feeling as if she were jumping feetfirst into a deep vat of icy water. "And it would be a challenge."

"Let me give you my card. Then you will know where to send the letter," Marie said. She fished in her reticule and brought out a small, gold-edged card and a purse which she pressed into Sparrow's hands. "I cannot convey my gratitude to you. And I am sure that I can trust you. Only find out for me if Adam is at Craig Bothwell and write immediately if he is. Then you may stay on there if you have obtained employment or return as it pleases you."

She flashed a sudden, grateful smile and hurried off, turning once to raise a gloved hand in salute.

It had to be a jest, Sparrow thought, looking at the card. In flowing script the name Marie Sinclair and the address she had given in Beaumont Gardens were inscribed. The purse was a neat black leather one. She opened it and shut it again quickly, seeing the glint of gold coins within. It seemed that Marie Sinclair had been absolutely serious in her request.

Thomas was emerging somewhat unsteadily from the tavern. Hastily she stuffed card and purse into her own reticule and went to meet him.

One thing was certain. She could not possibly confide the nature of her employment to Tizzie, who was already shocked at the notion of her charge becoming a temporary governess. She would certainly not countenance any such adventure as this. Sparrow was not in the least certain that she countenanced it herself. Chasing after an errant lover was surely an unladylike course of action. It could also be proof of a passionate and undying attachment. If so, then it looked as if all the passion was on the lady's side. Unless something really had happened to Adam Stuart. The novels she and Tizzie devoured frequently told of long-lost heirs held prisoner. Sparrow considered the possibility for a few moments, then discarded it. It was far more likely that Adam Stuart, having arrived at his great-uncle's house, had—like many young men before him—realised that distance didn't increase enchantment and been too craven to inform his beloved of his change of heart. She had been a pretty creature too, with her softly curling hair and her pleading brown eyes. Adam Stuart ought to have treated her with more honesty and tenderness.

By this time they had reached the house and she had to turn her efforts hastily to the provision of two stories, one for Tizzie and the other for her father. Her father was the easier to fool, partly because his leg was paining him too much to allow him to listen closely, partly because she had never told him a deliberate lie before.

"Augusta Hilton? I cannot recall your mentioning a schoolfellow of that name," he said, banged a pillow into shape with his elbow.

"I am sure you do, Father. She lives in Scotland and has written most kindly inviting me to visit her."

The possibility of his demanding to see the letter was

44

remote. It was Justin Harvey's boast that he had never read a book or a letter since leaving school though he did often glance through a newspaper to discover which two-year-olds were fancied or what that damned Boney was up to these days.

"I cannot spare Tizzie to go with you," he said. "Not that I am praising her qualities as a nurse for she has none, but left to Susan's tender mercies I will likely die of neglect."

"Travel arrangements are to be made for me," Sparrow said vaguely.

This was the dangerous moment since Justin, though a casual parent, was exceedingly fond of his daughter, and apt to become solicitous at the wrong juncture. Fortunately his injured limb reminded him of its existence at that instant by sending a stabbing pain into his foot that so took his attention away from Sparrow and beyond grumbling that in his opinion a girl ought to bestir herself to wed and not go galumphing up to the wild north that he let the matter drop.

To Sparrow's relief Tizzie too was inclined to accept her story at its face value without probing too minutely into its details.

"Scotland seems a very long way off to go merely for six weeks," she said only. "Can Mrs. Hilton not find a temporary governess nearer to home?"

"She is anxious lest her children grow up speaking with a Scottish accent," Sparrow said.

"How many children does she have?"

"Two. Adam and Stuart," Sparrow said, mentally crossing her fingers. She had never lied to Tizzie before either, but she regarded this occasion as justified because poor Tizzie had more than enough on her plate with the nursing of Justin.

"They are small then else they'd be away at school. I hope you can cope with two little boys," Tizzie said discouragingly. "Boys can be very difficult."

"They are delicate and not much given to mischief. And

the salary is very generous." She had already given Tizzie the fifty guineas in the purse.

"Their mother must be desperate to find someone if she's willing to pay before you even get there. I don't like your travelling alone on the stage though. Perhaps we should send Susan with you."

"Oh, Tizzie, how many governesses turn up with their personal maidservant in tow?" Sparrow objected.

"I suppose you are right," Tizzie conceded. "If you insist upon earning money, and I am not denying it's welcome, you could do worse than hire yourself out as a governess. Craig Bothwell. Never heard of it."

"Apparently the stage goes to the estate," Sparrow said.

"Well, be sure you write the moment you get there and if it's not a respectable house, you come back immediately."

She pressed five guineas into Sparrow's hand and went flustering up the stairs in response to Justin's irritable bellow.

Sparrow shook off a sudden feeling of nervousness. It was one thing to promise to do something for a complete stranger, quite another to find oneself on the verge of doing it. And she was far from happy about the tales she had spun to her father and Tizzie, though she salved her conscience to some extent by reminding herself that her motive was to spare them needless anxiety on her behalf.

The ringing of the doorbell made her jump and the sound of Henry's voice in the hall as Susan admitted him was a surprise. She had not expected to hear it for a long time.

"Good morning, Henry. How good of you to come." She greeted him calmly, scolding herself for the regret that pricked her at the sight of his pleasant face and neatly combed fair hair. He was a most eligible young bachelor and she was undoubtedly a fool to have relinquished him so readily.

"Sparrow, I have been thinking," he said.

"Oh?" She indicated a chair but he remained standing, clutching his hat.

"I have been thinking," he said, "that my conduct has not been that pertaining to a gentleman. A man has the right to choose his own bride. He cannot be influenced by whether or not his father is likely to be named as a peer."

"I suppose not," Sparrow said.

"I have decided that if you wish our engagement to be announced then I am ready to issue a notice to that effect, to inform my parents, and naturally seek your father's permission," Henry said.

It would be so easy to say yes, to take advantage of the sense of duty and honour that had brought him here. She would be able to cancel her pretended visit cum teaching post, to send back the fifty guineas, and persuade Henry it wasn't necessary to wait a year before they were married.

"It's very good of you," she said, speaking rapidly before she could change her mind, "but I don't believe we would suit at all. You will be much happier if you oblige your parents and pay court to Jane Marquis. Now, if you will excuse me, I am getting ready to go on a trip to visit an old school friend—"

"I came at an inconvenient time and expressed myself clumsily," he reproached himself.

"No indeed. My mind was quite made up. Thank you for asking me, Henry, but I think our decision not to wed was correct," she said firmly, opening the door and almost knocking Susan over.

"Mr. Fairfax is leaving. Good day to you, Henry."

"We must always be friends," he said.

"Yes indeed," she agreed and closed the door firmly.

Before she had time to draw a deep breath Susan had opened the door again, announcing, "Mr. Adair is here, Miss."

"Thank you, Susan. May I offer you some refreshment, Mr. Adair?"

She realised rather guiltily that she had offered Henry nothing.

"Nothing, thank you." He smiled at Susan, who bridled, blushed, and withdrew.

"I met Fairfax on his way out," Simon observed. "You look a little flustered."

"Henry proposed marriage to me," Sparrow told him.

"Oh?" Dark brows arched above the vivid, long-lashed eyes.

"He felt obliged to do so," she said in a small voice. "I refused him."

"I come with a request myself," Simon said.

"You are not going to propose marriage to me, are you?" she asked nervously.

"That is one question I have never asked," he said solemnly. "I am sorry if you had certain expectations, Miss Sparrow—"

"Indeed I had none." She interrupted him with some heat. "I really cannot understand what on earth made me say such a thing. I can only excuse myself by telling you that I do feel somewhat discomposed today. I am preparing to leave on a journey—but you had some request?"

"Merely to enquire the price of the saddle my man took away with the horse. It was not specified on the bill."

"Was it not? I never thought of that," Sparrow frowned, trying to sound businesslike. "How much would it be worth, d'ye think?"

"Ten guineas would be a fair price. It's well tooled."

"Why that's splendid!" Her small face lit up. "Since I learned of Father's reverses money has positively been pouring into the house."

"Oh?" He looked interested.

"The truth is—" Sparrow said and hesitated. She was not at all sure it would be wise to confide the exact truth to this harsh-featured young man with the teasing eyes. "The truth is that though my father believes I am going on a visit to an old school friend I am in reality entering a temporary situation."

"As what?"

"A governess. Two dear little boys up in Scotland." She was beginning to feel quite fond of her charges, she reflected. Adam had freckles and an impish grin. Stuart was the quiet one.

"Scotland!" There was a sudden sharpness in his voice. "That's an unconscionably long way off."

"Temporary situations are not so easily come by," she said defensively, "and as soon as my father is up and about again he will of course be able to recoup his recent losses."

"Meanwhile his pride is to be salvaged at all costs even though it means his daughter must travel into the wilderness among strangers?"

"You make it sound as if Scotland were at the North Pole," she retorted. "Anyway it is a challenge."

"When a nonswimmer is challenged to risk the water," he shot back, "he generally wades into a fairly shallow river. He doesn't dive headfirst into the depths of the Atlantic Ocean."

"Meaning you do not believe me capable of doing the job?"

"Miss Sparrow," he returned promptly, "any young lady who balances on balconies in order to throw down beef patties to a mudlark is capable of meeting any challenge. How will your orphans contrive to survive during your absence?"

"In the same way they survived before I came across them. I don't flatter myself that I am indispensable."

"Does your—the housekeeper know about the situation?"

"My chaperone, though she seldom acts as such since my father brought me up to be more independent than most ladies. Yes, of course she knows. She was doubtful at first, but I coaxed her to my way of thinking."

"I'm sure you did," he said with a faintly down-curving grin. "I suspect you have a silver tongue to match your eyes. Did you know how rare a truly grey eye is? Most so called have an admixture of blue or green, but yours are pure grey with that sparkle of silver in their depths that makes a man want to look closer."

Indeed he was suiting action to words, bending to gaze into her eyes until she could see her twin selves reflected in his pupils.

Close to, she could see how the black hair sprang from the broad forehead, the faint white scar that slashed the end of one eyebrow, the jutting nose and chin with the unexpectedly tender mouth between.

"You said ten guineas," she blurted, and retreated a step.

"So I did." The turquoise eyes were laughing at her. "Here you are, Miss Sparrow."

"I will give you a receipt." She went hastily to the small writing desk. "You can keep this with the bill of sale and then all is done correctly."

"You are not accustomed to writing?" he remarked, taking a step nearer again.

"I have been complimented on my penmanship," she said, irritated. "Why?"

"Your hand is trembling," he pointed out. "I thought unfamiliarity with the pen might be the cause."

"It is somewhat chilly in here. There, Mr. Adair, is your receipt."

"Very pretty penmanship," he approved, running his eye over it. "You will be an asset to any household up in Scotland. How do you travel there?"

"By stage—and I have my packing to complete, so I must ask you to excuse me now."

"Alone by stage. When you take up a challenge you don't stint yourself, do you?"

"It is a matter of necessity, Mr. Adair."

"It is a pity we are not related, then you could call me by my given name. Simon and Sparrow blend well together, don't you think?"

"Not particularly." She was surprised into a giggle. "They sound like a firm of solicitors."

"Simon and Sparrow—Simon being the senior partner, of course."

"And Sparrow the more brilliant."

"Far be it from me to contradict a lady. This is for luck."

As her hand found the doorknob he bent and kissed her swiftly on the cheek. Her first response was of indignation that he should salute her on such short acquaintance. Following on that and blazing shame into her cheeks was the regret that he had not kissed her for a longer time in a different place. That was the most unladylike wish she had ever had and she was furious with them both.

"Give my love to Bonnie Scotland," Simon Adair said, and passed into the hall before she could utter one cutting remark.

=== 4 ===

HER TRUNK WAS packed, tissue between each layer. Sparrow sat on the end of her bed threading string through the labels.

Miss S. Harvey
Craig Bothwell
Scotland

It was a romantic-sounding address anyway, she reflected. She wondered if she would be able to obtain some sort of employment there.

"Now be sure to write and let me know how you are coping with the little boys," Tizzie had warned. "Don't take any nonsense from them, mind."

"No, indeed I won't," Sparrow had assured her, mentally crossing her fingers for the tenth time. "I shall be very firm."

"At least it's only for a short time," Tizzie consoled them both. "There's no denying that the money will be useful. You know I did think we might take in lodgers, but these days one cannot be too careful. And your father wouldn't much like strangers in the house."

"He would absolutely hate it," Sparrow said decidedly. "No, you concentrate on nursing him, and don't worry about me. I shall enjoy the adventure."

"I did hope that Mr. Henry would come put to scratch and make an offer," Tizzie said wistfully.

"We wouldn't have suited," Sparrow said briefly.

"Well, there was always something a bit mean-looking

about his mouth," Tizzie said unfairly, and took herself off at a bellow from Justin.

Tying the labels to the handle of the small trunk and the bandbox, Sparrow contemplated their contents with some misgiving. Tizzie had packed most of her garments, insisting on putting in two evening gowns.

"If they ever do have a ball, dearie, then the governess will certainly be expected to attend and you don't want to look frumpish."

Sparrow had a shrewd suspicion that governesses were expected to look frumpish more often than not. In any event she was more likely to obtain work as a kitchen maid and she was sure they were not expected to attend balls. Neither, she suspected, did they arrive from the south by stagecoach on the off chance of possible employment.

She reminded herself firmly that she was already employed—to find Adam Stuart, Marie Sinclair's missing fiance. She couldn't help feeling that Marie Sinclair displayed a rather feeble spirit in sending someone else to look for him, but not all young ladies craved adventure and the situation did appear to be a somewhat delicate one.

In a way it was a pity she couldn't confide in her father, but for all his breezy and unconventional attitude to the world at large there were certain things at which Justin Harvey drew the line in his daughter's case, and Tizzie would certainly not approve. The labels secured she slipped a cape over her dress and went down to the front hall. Tizzie was reading bits of sporting news out of one of the newspapers to Justin, who was interrupting with ribald comments from time to time, and Susan was in the kitchen. There was time for a walk before darkness fell. Exercise was necessary when one was going to spend two days cooped up in the stage, Sparrow advised herself, not stopping to ask herself the real cause of her restlessness.

The park was in full flower, bushes cascading blossom over the narrow gravel paths, a few nursemaids lingering to savour the last warmth of the sun. The round pond glittered and gleamed, with two small boys sailing a boat across its surface. It was unusual for young ladies to stroll unescorted, but Sparrow frequently went to the park, where it was possible to relish an hour's solitude or walk off a bad mood.

Today she would have appreciated a companion, someone to exchange remarks with about the beauty of the setting or the journey that lay ahead of her. The problem was, she told herself, that she was missing Henry. She had grown accustomed to him. Soon, she supposed, he would marry Jane Marquis, and she would continue to walk alone in the park.

She sat down on one of the benches that were scattered at intervals within the railed grounds and stared somewhat forlornly at the glittering pond. The sun was turning to fire and sinking slowly into ashes, and a pale moon was already outlined faintly in the sky. A voice called and the two small boys hastily pulled out their dripping boat and ran past her across the grass.

Someone was watching her. Sparrow felt the hairs at the nape of her neck prickle slightly as her sharp ears caught a rustle in the bushes. There were pickpockets around especially at the latter end of the day. Tizzie had caught one once and soundly boxed his ears. Turning her head sharply she met a pair of bright eyes peering at her from beneath a tangled fringe.

"What do you want?" She asked the question crossly, irritated by her own nervous reaction, as the grubby urchin pushed his way clear of the bushes.

"You going away somewhere?" he demanded.

"Yes—and how do you know? Have you been eavesdropping?" She fixed the mudlark with an icy frown.

"Heard your coachman talking, didn't I?" the boy said rhetorically. "Going to Scotland to visit friends, he said, and not likely to be coming back in a 'urry. Ain't you wedding the posh gentleman then?"

"If you mean Mr. Henry Fairfax," Sparrow said repressively, "then no I am not."

"Some folks spit on their luck," the boy said in disgust. "If you don't wed 'im then what am I supposed to do for vittles?"

"If you imagine that my marriage to Mr. Fairfax would have ensured you an endless supply of beef patties," she said with dignity, "then you are grossly mistaken."

"You use awful long words," he said plaintively. "Never mind, you've a good 'eart."

"Thank you for that—what's your name by the by?"

"Lancelot," the boy informed her.

"Oh no it isn't," Sparrow said firmly.

"Yes, it is," he said doggedly. "Lancelot Higgindrop. I was born legal and dipped in the font over St. Clement's way."

"And your parents?"

"My mother died when I was a baby and my dad drank hisself into the grave after her," he told her. "Sad, ain't it?"

"Very sad—if it's true."

"It's true all right." He brushed some clinging leaves off his tattered person and squatted at her feet. "Who was Lancelot, Miss?"

"A very brave gentleman who fell in love with Queen Guinevere," she informed him.

"Crikey!" He screwed up his grimy little face in disgust. "Was that all he did?"

"I believe he fought a few battles," Sparrow admitted.

"That sounds more like it." He looked encouraged at the idea.

"When you are grown up you can fight battles too, perhaps," Sparrow said.

"I'm grown up now," her companion told her. "I'm past thirteen."

"You only look about ten."

"That's lack of feeding," he said in a matter-of-fact way. "Some old cove tells me once I could go to sea as a cabin boy, but I never fancied it. When the press-gangs are out I get under my bridge and stay there. Nobody's dragging me off to be killed by the Frenchies!"

"Very brave of you," Sparrow said.

"No it ain't. It's dead cowardly," he contradicted. "Did you know someone's casing your house?"

"Casing?" Sparrow looked at him.

"Watching it with a view to getting in and cleaning—robbing the place."

"Who?" she asked with a tremor of alarm.

"Don't know 'is name," the other said regretfully. "Black-'aired gent who collared me that time you was at the Fairfax place."

"Simon Adair?" Sparrow looked at him in astonishment and then laughed. "Oh, Mr. Adair escorted me home that night."

"At two in the mornin'?"

"No, of course not," Sparrow said.

"Well, at two in the morning he was there all right, riding slow up and down the road. I saw 'im with me own eyes and I knowed it was two 'cos the church clock struck," Lancelot told her. "Then off he goes like a greaser when he sees a copper's nark."

"And what were you doing outside the house at two in the morning?" she enquired.

"Takin' a stroll," Lancelot said with an innocent air.

"You will end up on the gallows," Sparrow said severely.

"Not if you keep 'elping me," he said sweetly. "But with you up in Scotland I might not make it."

She did not, of course, believe one word he said, though there really wasn't any reason for him to invent the earlier part of his story. And no reason, she thought, for Simon to have returned in the middle of the night in order to ride up and down the street.

"I have five shillings," she said aloud, bringing her mind back to more immediate problems. "I will give it to you on condition you spend it on food—not gin."

"That I'll never do," Lancelot said with such emphasis that she was inclined to believe him. "I remember my old dad going that road—straight to the knacker's yard."

"Very well then." Sparrow opened her purse and took out the five coins. "I do not expect to be many weeks in

Scotland, so try to keep out of trouble until I get back." She considered the notion of asking Tizzie to keep a watch and slip the lad some food now and then, but discarded it. Neither Tizzie nor Susan had much sympathy with the undeserving poor.

"You can call me Lance if you like, Miss," the boy said.

"Thank you, Lance," she said gravely. "You may call me Miss Sparrow—my name is Sparrow."

"Yes, Miss. I'm sorry about that, Miss," Lance said sympathetically and was gone, the coins clutched in his fist, before she could open her mouth.

It was getting very dusky now and a chill wind ruffled her hair. She pulled up her hood and started for home, quickening her steps as she realised that the park was deserted. Even in this genteel district it was not wise for a female to walk alone after dark. To her annoyance the gates leading to the crescent were already locked. That meant she would have to go round to the side gate, which, for some reason, the keeper never troubled to secure. She took a firmer hold of her reticule and walked briskly, wishing her skirts were fuller so that she could take longer steps.

She had almost reached the gates when voices on the other side of the wall caused her to pause. A man's voice and then the lighter tones of a woman. The man's voice she knew, though he was speaking low and rapidly. The few words she caught were French.

"*Il est possible mais je ne sais—*"

And the light voice answering, "*Ah, mignon, tu es un—*"

Footsteps and the voices faded. Sparrow waited a second and then softly unlatched the gate and stuck out her head into the narrow alley behind.

The couple were walking away towards the curricle that stood at the top of the alley. A tiger in the striped livery of his calling held the horses, so presumably the pair had taken a short walk in order to discuss private matters. Very private if they were also taking the precaution of speaking in French. Sparrow's own French was better than the usual

57

schoolgirl variety since her father, who knew the country well, had insisted on speaking the language to her frequently. In this instance her fluency had availed her little beyond the knowledge that the lady had addressed Adair as "darling." Which was certainly not the reason, Sparrow told herself irritably, she felt so cross as she stared after the retreating couple. Though the last of the light had almost vanished, she recognised the towering plumes on the high-piled hair of the lady into whose curricle she had seen Simon Adair climb. The lady was clearly an intimate companion. She refused to speculate how intimate. What was interesting was that he was still in the neighbourhood. She wondered if Lance—ridiculous name—had been correct in his assumption that Simon Adair was watching the house. If so he was surely not interested in robbing it. And if he did, she thought with a quiver of amusement, there wasn't much that was valuable for him to take. They had reached the curricle. The slim figure with the plumed hat turned, Simon Adair bent his head. Sparrow stepped hastily within the gate again, her cheeks burning as if she were the one being soundly kissed.

The rattling of harness and the trotting of hooves told her that it was safe to venture out again. The curricle was diminishing into the distance. Sparrow turned in the other direction, fixing her mind firmly on other matters.

It was sad to realise that in a civilised country in the year eighteen hundred and eleven there were thousands of children like Lance who slept in hovels and under bridges and in the porches of churches, scraping an existence either by doing hard, dirty work or by stealing. The journey up to Scotland on the morrow would provide plenty in the way of scenic variety; it almost seemed unfair to leave Tizzie with the nursing of a reluctant invalid while she herself was setting out on what promised to be an exciting quest. And why had Simon Adair been kissing that dreadful woman? She had to be dreadful, Sparrow decided illogically, to wear such enormous feathers in her hat.

She gained her own front door without incident and went in to a scolding from Susan. "I was fretting about you, Miss, honest I was. Why, you might have had your throat cut or your purse snatched. There's no telling what might happen when a respectable girl goes out these days. It's all that Bonaparte's fault, you know?"

"How?" Sparrow enquired, divesting herself of her cape and wrenching her mind from questions about kissing.

"He makes people nervous," Susan said darkly, "and when people get nervous they start acting strange, not according to law."

"I'm sure you have a point there, Susan," Sparrow said, amused, and went on up to the stairs to her father's room.

The invalid was sitting up in bed, a cage over his splinted leg, his colour somewhat less ruddy than usual, but otherwise showing little sign of damage.

"Where the devil have you been?" he enquired as his daughter tapped on the door and entered.

"Taking a walk, Papa." Sparrow bent to kiss his cheek, sniffed, and added, "And you have been drinking rum again. You know it gives you heartburn."

"Took a mouthful to wash down the medicine," he growled. "If I'm going to get heartburn then I may as well have it while I'm already suffering. Who is this new young man Tizzie has been gabbling about?"

"No new young man," Sparrow said. "Mr. Adair was kind enough to escort me home the other night and good enough to take Sultan off your hands."

"Selling my horse without a by-your-leave," he grumbled. "I'd have mastered him in the end, you know. Never been a horse or a woman I couldn't tame."

"Except me," Tizzie said, coming in. "Sparrow, where did you get to?"

"I went for a walk in the park."

"At this hour? Mr. Harvey, speak to her!"

"Don't do it," Justin said.

"For heaven's sake," Sparrow said, forgetting to be cautious. "You make a fuss about a walk in the park and tomorrow I'm off up to Scotland and staying overnight at a strange place."

"I hadn't considered that." Her father frowned.

"Oh, the stage is very safe," Sparrow said hastily. "Safer than the park, actually."

"Tizzie, pass me that flat box in the top drawer," he ordered.

Tizzie gave him a doubtful look but obeyed, laying the flat, rectangular case on the bed.

"I gave this to your mother when we were first married," Justin said, lifting the lid. "Very neat and small enough to fit in a lady's reticule."

"Why on earth did you give her a pistol?" Sparrow stared at the tiny, pearl-handled weapon.

"I promised her that if I proved to be a bad husband she could shoot me. Fortunately, I never gave her the occasion. Pick it up, girl. It won't bite you."

She picked it up gingerly.

"Oh, do be careful," Tizzie begged, backing off. "I never did hold with those nasty things."

"It isn't loaded," Justin informed her. "The bullets are here. Three bullets, Sparrow, so you can shoot three people if it's ever necessary. I'll show you how to load, cock, aim, and fire. Then you can feel perfectly at ease while you're on your way to Scotland."

It was on the tip of her tongue to refuse, but a second thought held her back. It was just barely possible that some harm had befallen Marie Sinclair's fiancé, in which case the possession of a gun might just prove very convenient. She couldn't imagine herself ever shooting anybody, but the very fact that she had the means to do so might give her more confidence.

"That's very good of you, Father," she said brightly. "I shall take great care of them."

"I never heard of such a thing," Tizzie said in a flouncing manner.

"Hold your tongue and go tell Susan to hurry up with the supper," Justin growled. "And no pap. I fancy a nice beefsteak pie."

"What we fancy," said Tizzie, leaving the room with dignity, "we don't always receive."

"That's a good woman," he mused, gazing after her. "An invaluable woman, Sparrow. Without her, you and I would be sunk deep. Now give me the pistol and I'll show you how it works. After all, Scotland is a considerable distance off, and they're all Jacobites up there still from what I hear."

"Bonnie Prince Charlie died years ago," Sparrow reminded him.

"No matter," her father said darkly. "The Scots have long memories. Now pay attention."

Sparrow paid attention. By the time Tizzie returned with a poached salmon and a dish of roast parsnips on a tray she had mastered the simple techniques of loading, cocking, and aiming, though her attacker, she thought, would have to be obliging enough to stand perfectly still while she was doing all that.

"Better not waste a bullet by firing it," Justin said with a reluctant note in his voice.

"I should think not," Tizzie said indignantly. "I certainly don't wish to have a hole in the ceiling. Now put the nasty thing away. Sparrow, your supper is downstairs if you'll be so good. I intend to stay and see Mr. Harvey eats every bite."

"Tyrant!" Justin said and attacked his salmon with gusto.

Sparrow went downstairs slowly, clutching her reticule in which pistol and bullets now resided, wrapped in a silk cloth. For all its small size the weapon felt heavy. She tried, and failed, to imagine herself actually firing it at someone.

Halfway through her salmon and parsnips she decided, with an involuntary giggle, that she could probably bring herself to shoot tall plumes off a fashionable hat.

Morning brought a bright, sunny day. It was the kind of day when all things seem possible. She donned her plainest travelling dress, tied the ribbons of her straw bonnet firmly, and went upstairs to bid her father goodbye.

"Now have a pleasant visit with your friend," he warned, "don't go falling in love with any Scotsman, and kindly bear in mind that while you are enjoying yourself I am trapped on a bed of pain with a dragon in charge."

"Nonsense, you and Tizzie will get along famously," Sparrow rallied him. "I promise to enjoy myself and not to stay too long."

The thought that she might find Adam Stuart immediately and not need to find any temporary employment occurred to her. She would have to remain away for a month at least, or invent a tale to explain the terrible event that had occasioned her speedy return. "Father, my school friend eloped with the butcher and her family struck out her name." "Oh, Tizzie, the house had burned down and everybody perished in the flames."

Putting on her cloak she decided gloomily that at the rate she was going she would end up a habitual liar.

"Now you turn right round and come home again," Tizzie warned as Sparrow went out to the carriage, "if they don't treat you with respect. You make sure those children understand they have to behave."

"I swear. Take care of Father and yourself," Sparrow said.

Now that the moment for leaving had arrived she suddenly wanted to stay where she was and inform Henry that she had changed her mind. She quelled the temptation sternly and entered the carriage.

The stage was already being loaded when they reached the posting station, and a crowd of people bustled about, some saying their farewells to relatives and friends, others checking their tickets.

"If you will see to the luggage," Sparrow told Thomas, "I will collect my ticket."

A great many people had apparently decided to travel north. She was forced to use the tip of her parasol once or twice before she could clear a path for herself through the crowd.

"Miss Harvey?"

The clerk at the counter of the ticket office nodded.

"Ticket for you, Miss, and a letter."

He handed both over. Sparrow put the ticket in her purse and stepped aside to open the bulky letter. The promised fifty guineas were there, wrapped securely in a handkerchief, together with a single sheet of paper on which a few lines were scrawled.

Dear Miss Harvey,

My grateful thanks for your help. If you find my fiancé do please be so good as not to tell him that you are seeking him on my behalf. It is, I fear, a most unlikely proceeding for a female to undertake. Gentlemen do not like to be pursued. I am sure I can rely on your tact and discretion.

Gratefully Yours—M.S.

A shadow fell across the page.

"If you don't make haste," Simon Adair said, "you will lose your seat."

Sparrow jumped violently and dropped the handkerchief, sending guineas rolling over the floor.

"Not a very safe way to carry your money," Simon said severely, bending to pick up the errant coins. "I think that—"

"I like to be able to get at them quickly," Sparrow said, flustered. She had hastily crumpled up the letter and slipped it into the top of her parasol. "And I really cannot imagine what you are doing. If you've come to see me off that's very kind of you but really quite unnecess—"

"I merely chanced to be here." He had straightened up, and now raised his head from the handkerchief he had picked up from the floor. "Yours?"

"Thank you." She took the handkerchief and began to wrap up the coins again, conscious of his brooding blue gaze. After a moment he said, "I wish you a pleasant journey, Miss Harvey."

There was an almost indefinable change in his manner. She felt it keenly without, however, being able to analyse or explain it. Now he was lifting his hat as ceremoniously as if he had never seen her perched on a balcony and walking away. She stared after him, biting her lip. It was stupid but she suddenly felt forlorn.

"Your bag is aboard, Miss," Thomas announced, shouldering his way through the crowd.

"Thank you, Thomas." She made her way to the stage, lifted her hand in farewell, and climbed aboard, squeezing herself into the narrow space between the window and a stout matron with a large basket on her arm. From the glares the lady was getting from passengers who were colliding with the basket as they sought their sets, Sparrow deduced that her companion was liable to be exceedingly unpopular before she reached her destination.

The great vehicle swayed out of the yard with the horn blaring. The passengers who rode on top would be clinging tightly as it rounded the corner and entered the main road, the usual complement of urchins running after it and catcalling as the horn sounded the off.

Sparrow leaned back against the upholstered seat and tried to work out why Simon Adair's manner had changed so abruptly. He had become positively glacial for no reason at all. She frowned, picturing him with his head bent over the handkerchief in which the coins had been wrapped. Something about the handkerchief had displeased him?

The bulk of the stout lady shielded her from the gaze of the other passengers. Turning her shoulder slightly Sparrow fumbled in her reticule and succeeded in untying the knot, tipping the coins with a series of tiny clinks into the interior of her reticule, and extracting the square of white silk.

It was, as far as she could tell, a perfectly adequate handkerchief, a monogram embroidered in black silk at one corner. A tied bow with the ends tucked under. Sparrow gave up the struggle to understand, pushed the handkerchief with everything else now in her bulging reticule, and tried to concentrate on the passing scene and not listen to the stout woman, who was informing the entire uninterested compartment that she was taking some home-cooked pies along for her daughter-in-law in York since the latter had a bad back and suffered something chronic with her feet.

York, Sparrow, reflected, seemed an awfully long way off. She fixed her eyes on the streets but they had soon left the city behind and were bowling at high speed along the main London-to-York road.

It ought to have been an interesting drive, since the day was fine and the passing scenery varied greatly but her mind was bursting with other problems. There was Simon Adair, who popped up everywhere and whose manners were, at the least, mercurial; there was Henry, who really would make a very satisfactory husband; there was the missing Adam Stuart, whose sweetheart was so anxious for news of him that she had trusted a complete stranger with one hundred guineas; there was the unwelcome knowledge that her father hadn't any money and didn't own the house she had regarded as home for the past six years; there was a dark lady in a feathered hat who talked in French and kissed gentlemen practically on the public highway.

They stopped briefly for a change of horses and a ten-minute break to enable the passengers to stretch their legs and then they were bowling northward again. Sparrow had begun to feel exceedingly hungry and thirsty. Tizzie, probably thinking there would be longer pauses along the way, had neglected to provide any refreshments.

"It's very good eel pie, my dear, though I say it as shouldn't." The stout lady was holding out a large slice wrapped in a napkin.

"That's very good of you," Sparrow said, changing her opinion of her companion. "My—I forgot to bring anything to eat or drink, I'm afraid."

"First time by stage? Ah, I make the trip every year," the other said. "Very young to be travelling alone."

Sparrow, guessing correctly that the lady was referring to her and not to her own mature person, said meekly, "I am travelling to Scotland to see a friend, ma'am. This is my first long journey."

"Eat up and I'll pour some cider, if this dratted coach will hold itself upright long enough for me to manage it without spilling. There, now. No need to fret, sir. I am certain that only a drop actually went on your trousers, so don't scowl at me so. Scowling makes lines in the face, as I am forever telling my daughter-in-law."

Sparrow munched the eel pie and drank the cider, studiously avoiding the indignant eyes of the gentleman seated opposite whose trousers had just been baptised with a splash from the bottle of cider.

The day wore on, even the stout woman ceasing her litany in order to lean back her head and snore gently. Late that night they were due to reach York where some passengers would disembark and those who were going on over the border would stay at the coaching inn, the price of the night's lodging being included in the ticket.

Another brief stop at late afternoon gave another opportunity for a brisk walk up and down to relieve cramped limbs. Sparrow held tightly to her reticule, thinking that it would avail her nothing to be carrying a pistol were the coach to be held up by highwaymen. She would have to pull out the handkerchief and all the guineas, unwrap the weapon, and request them to stand still while she loaded, cocked, and took aim. The picture amused her so much that a trill of amusement escaped her and was answered by an echoing giggle from the coach. Intrigued, Sparrow stepped nearer, craning her neck to look up at the luggage rack with its assortment of trunks and boxes.

"Oh, no!" She closed her eyes and shook her head, willing what she had just seen to be gone when she looked again.

It was not. Lancelot Higgindrop peered down at her from among the piled baggage, his mouth split in a wide grin under the tangle of hair.

"Hello, Miss Sparrow," he greeted her cheerfully. "You ain't 'alf got a catching laugh."

"Lance, what are you doing here?" she demanded.

"Travelling to Scotland," he informed her, scrambling

down. "And I paid for me seat up top same as everyone else. With the five shillings you give me."

"Which was for food."

"Which wasn't for gin, and I ain't spent it on gin."

"You have been very careful to keep out of sight until now," she chided. "What on earth do you want to travel into Scotland for? I certainly cannot look out for you. I am going to be very busy indeed about other affairs."

"Maybe I'll be looking out for you," he said. "I seen that Simon Adair at the posting station. Following you again. I reckon you need someone to take an eye out. And you can't send me back 'cos it's too far to walk and there ain't no stage for a couple of days."

"Then you must make shift for yourself," Sparrow said. "I certainly don't wish—look, you cannot arrive in Scotland without anything at all. You better take this guinea and don't expect any more. When the return coach leaves I shall expect you to be on it."

She thrust the coin into his hand and snapped her purse shut, walking back to the stage with the uncomfortable feeling that she had just acquired one more problem.

= 5 =

BY THE TIME the stage rolled into York the sun had long since set and dark clouds were rolling in from the west. Sparrow had hoped to see something of the city but she saw only the cobbled yard of the posting inn and the slender spire of the minster against the star-glinted sky before she was swept along with the other passengers into the hostelry.

Supper was welcome and tasty, eaten at a long table round which those continuing their journey on into Scotland gathered. The stout woman had taken herself and her basket off, and there was no sign of Lance. Sparrow guessed that he had probably found a way to cadge free vittles in the kitchen. Then she reminded herself firmly that he wasn't her responsibility and, having finished her steak and kidney pudding and drunk her mug of ale, she requested a passing maidservant to point out her room.

She had been fortunate to have been allotted a room to herself, not a large chamber but one that looked warm and clean. Having secured the door, she removed her outer garments, washed her face in the water provided, and lay thankfully down to sleep.

At six the next morning a tap on the door brought the maidservant with fresh hot water and the information that the stage would leave at seven sharp. So far, so good, Sparrow thought as she made her ablutions. Apart from Lance's unexpected arrival the trip had been uneventful. She went down to the public dining-room feeling already like a seasoned traveller.

A few newcomers had joined the stage when she climbed back inside it after an ample breakfast of bacon, sausages, mushrooms, eggs, tomatoes, and scrambled cheese with kidneys. Two gentlemen with strong Scottish accents were evidently returning home after a trip south, and a tall, thin old lady informed everybody that she planned to attend her son's wedding in Edinburgh.

Sparrow set herself to enjoy the changing panorama unfolding beyond the windows. The roads were narrower and steeper now, not as well maintained as the southern route. She glimpsed several potholes as the stage rolled along, the sound of the horses' snorting as they toiled up each incline very audible in the crisp morning air.

At Carlisle there was a long halt with a luncheon served that was as ample as the breakfast. She caught sight of Lance, his cheek distended by an apple he was eating, and then the horn was sounding again and they were clambering inside the stage, which was becoming as familiar to her as her own chamber.

The country was becoming wilder as they penetrated further into the north. Sparrow could see long sweeps of heather-clad glen interspersed with pine and fir trees growing sparsely below the rock-crested hills. Now and then they travelled through a village, thatched huts of wattle and daub flinging her back centuries. Ragged, barefoot children ran out to wave at the passing stage. Once she glimpsed a pack of hounds in full cry after a fleeting red form and heard the far-off bugle of the huntsmen.

"Craig Bothwell!"

She was roused from a doze by the loud announcement of the coachman, who was peering in at the window. The coach had stopped and her trunk was being unloaded from the pile of luggage strapped aloft.

"Yes." She bestirred herself, climbing down into the road, still blinking sleep out of her eyes as the coachman remounted and the stage moved off in a cloud of dust.

"What now, Miss?" Lance emerged from the dust, grinning up at her trustingly.

"You would have done better to remain aboard until the stage reached Edinburgh," she said severely.

"Ain't this where your friend lives then?" He indicated the high walls and the closed iron gates that confronted them.

"Lance, I am not actually going to visit a friend," she began awkwardly.

"But you said—"

"Never mind what I said. The truth is that I am seeking a temporary post, for a few weeks only. I have sufficient to do with looking after myself but since you are here—"

"Since I am here," he said in a fair imitation of her refined accents, "we might as well stick together, eh?"

"I was afraid you might say that," Sparrow said gloomily. "Come along then." She bent to pick up her trunk but Lance seized it first, hoisting it up with a strength that belied his undersized frame.

The gates were latched but not locked. Opening them and conscientiously closing them again after they had passed through, Sparrow looked up a long winding driveway with banks of gorse and fern at each side. At the end of the drive a turreted house of handsome proportions stood with a semi-circle of lawn round which a gravel path had been raked.

"Whatever made you fix on this place?" Lance demanded. "Did you 'ear as how they was wanting help?"

"It's too long a tale to explain now," Sparrow said. Her spirits, instead of rising at the sight of the trim, well-tended grounds and the large house with its many sparkling windows, were sinking. This was clearly an establishment occupied by wealthy, respectable people who would regard her sudden arrival in search of employment as highly eccentric. The presence of the boy wouldn't aid her situation either. She was casting about in her mind for some way to be rid of him when he said unexpectedly, "You won't get far with me along of you, Miss. Reckon I'll walk on into the village and get something there."

"What village?" Sparrow demanded.

"Bound to be a village," he said philosophically. "Stands to reason, don't it? I'll see you later, Miss."

He put down her trunk, lifted his hand in a salute, and scampered off.

Sparrow bit her lip. She had not desired Lance's company but now that he had taken himself off she felt curiously vulnerable. She reminded herself that Marie Sinclair had paid her a hundred guineas to find out what, if anything, had happened to Adam Stuart, and bent to pick up the trunk.

"There you are at last. Well, come along then, girl. Don't stand there like a ninny." Across the lawn came a tall woman in hooped skirts and high-piled powdered hair, looking as if she had just stepped out of a time thirty years before.

"Ma'am," Sparrow said in bewilderment.

"You may call me Lady Agnes," the other said with the air of conferring a particular favour.

"Lady Agnes," Sparrow said.

"You should have made the boy carry your luggage right up to the door," the lady scolded.

"Yes, I—" Sparrow hesitated, wondering what on earth to say next.

"I take it that you have a name," Lady Agnes was continuing as Sparrow lugged the trunk along. "Miss Marchmont never said. Foolish woman, to break her leg before she had even set out on the journey. However, at least she had the sense to send a replacement."

"It seems to be the season for breaking legs," Sparrow commented.

"What a very odd remark," the other said in a pleased tone. "I do so like oddities."

"I only meant that my father recently broke his own leg," Sparrow panted.

They had reached the shallow flight of steps that led up to the front door, and she dearly longed to relinquish the heavy trunk, but Lady Agnes was sweeping ahead, pushing open the door. Rather to her surprise Sparrow found herself in a large hall, panelled in light wood, with a cheerful red carpet snaking up the staircase and bunches of dyed grasses arranged in copper vases on a long table.

"Oh, it's very modern," she exclaimed.

"Isn't it though?" the other echoed. "Mind you, the house is only about a century old, but my husband adores new-fangled inventions—hot baths and indoor privies and all that nonsense, you know."

"You prefer the old," Sparrow hazarded.

"I prefer that which is most becoming," Lady Agnes retorted. "And you have still not told me your name. All that Marchmont creature told me was that she was providing a replacement until she was well enough to travel north."

"I'm Sparrow Harvey, Lady Agnes." And God bless the Marchmont creature for breaking her leg and providing a replacement. As to what would happen when the genuine replacement arrived she did not allow herself to speculate.

"Sparrow—what an odd name." Lady Agnes paused at the foot of the staircase and stared at her. "You are far too pretty to be a companion to a bad-tempered old woman like myself, you know. However, as it's only until the March-mont arrives then we shall just have to endure each other. Leave your trunk there. Angus will carry it up later. Come along."

Her panniered skirts rustled up the red carpet with Sparrow following. Lady Agnes was old, but her back was ramrod straight, and above a beaky nose her eyes were still sharp. She might be eccentric, Sparrow reflected, but she obviously was nobody's fool.

Making a right turn on the upper landing the old lady entered a long, sunlit gallery with windows along one side and what appeared to be various family portraits along the other. At the far end an archway led into a narrower passage with doors opening off it.

"The West Wing," Lady Agnes said, capitalising the words. "Much of it is occupied by myself. Sir Alasdair sleeps in the East Wing. Snores, you know. An excellent husband in almost every way but snores dreadfully. Has a temper too, but we need not consider that. This is your room. Angus will bring up your trunk and Morag will bring you hot water. Dinner is at seven, and you may begin your duties tomorrow."

With which pronouncement she closed the door firmly.

Sparrow gazed round her with interest, relieved to find that her new environment was both spacious and cheerful. There were patterned rugs on the floor that echoed the lemon and grey of the flocked wallpaper and a capacious bed in addition to a wardrobe, a dressing table, and a comfortable-looking chair. She was weary of sitting after the long hours in the stage, however, and so took a turn or two about the room, then went over to the large picture window and looked down into a garden planted with herbs laid out in a maze pattern that resembled a tapestry she had seen once in a museum. Beyond the hedge rose a squat tower, with slits that evidently served as windows. The stone of the building was covered with reddish creeper and it appeared to be deserted.

"Your baggage, Miss." A voice at the door prompted her to open it and admit a short, grizzled man in tartan trews who carried her trunk into the room, followed by a carroty-haired girl bearing a steaming pitcher.

"Thank you—Angus?"

"Angus Og, Miss," he nodded. "This is my daughter, Morag."

Morag dropped a curtsey as her father went out again. "Her Ladyship says you're to go down for the meal when the gong sounds," she said in a pleasantly lilting voice. "The dining-room's at the left, Miss, off the hall. It used to be the banqueting hall in the old days when Sir Alasdair and Her Ladyship were first wed, but there haven't been guests there for a long time. Would you be having everything you need?"

"I think so, thank you." Sparrow hesitated, then asked, "I was wondering what that building is over there beyond the garden?"

"Oh, that's the old keep," Morag said. "The family lived there before this house was built."

"It looks rather a grim dwelling," Sparrow commented.

"They didn't reckon much to comfort in those days," Morag said. "Nasty old place but Sir Alasdair felt it ought to be left. Would there be anything more you'll require now?"

"Not just now. Thank you, Morag."

"The bell's there if you do," the girl said pleasantly. "I'll away to the kitchen now to help my mother with the rest of the cooking."

"The whole family works here then?"

"Oh, there have been Ogs working for the Stuarts of Craig Bothwell for hundreds of years," Morag said. "Excuse me now, or you'll never be getting your dinner." She strode out, looking with her mane of carroty hair and her long legs as if she would have been more at home stalking deer on the heathery slopes.

At least she seemed chatty and friendly. As soon as the chance came Sparrow decided she would broach the subject of Adam Stuart to the girl. She hoped the chance would present itself before very long since it was more than likely that the real replacement for Miss Marchmont would arrive on the next coach. Meanwhile she availed herself of the welcome hot water to effect a more thorough toilet and unpacked her trunk, changing her thick travelling dress for a lighter gown of white woven wool with dark green ribbons under the high waistline and at the tight cuffs. She had no experience, but trusted that companions were expected to clothe themselves more fashionably than governesses.

By the time she was ready the light was fast fading, imparting an even more desolate aspect to the tower beyond the box hedge of the herb garden. When the sonorous notes of a gong reverberated through the house she tucked a green shawl about her slim shoulders and went out into the corridor. Lady Agnes must have gone down ahead of her since nobody emerged from any of the other doors, and she made her solitary way through the gallery and down the stairs where Morag stood next to a large brass gong which she had been sounding.

"On your left, Miss," she said with a smile and vanished through a baize-covered door at the back of the hall.

The door on the left was partly open and a masculine voice with a stronger Scottish burr than the well-bred tones of Lady Agnes was issuing forth.

"—and there's nae reason in bringing strangers to the house at the very time that—"

Sparrow tapped on the door and coughed politely.

"Ah, Sparrow Harvey, I take it?" The door was held wider by a gentleman whom Sparrow assumed was Sir Alasdair himself. He confirmed her supposition a moment later by saying, "I'm Sir Alasdair, young lady, and I hope you drink good whiskey and not the namby-pamby sherry wine that females pour down their throats these days."

"I don't often get good whiskey, Sir Alasdair," Sparrow said, amused, "but my father taught me to appreciate it when I do."

"For that you will have a wee dram with your dinner," he said, his gruff tone softening. He was a handsome old man with a shock of white hair and piercing grey eyes under bushy brows. A strong old man too, Sparrow surmised, noting the breadth of the shoulders under the jacket, the commanding height, the large, veined hands with their knotty joints.

"Shall we eat?" Lady Agnes said. "The child must be starving."

They were standing in a small anteroom and she turned as she spoke to throw open double doors which led into a huge, vaulted chamber beyond. In contrast to the rooms Sparrow had already seen, these had walls of stone, with rugs of skin and fur instead of patterned carpet on the floor, and massively carved furniture that showed the patina of age.

"Please be seated, Sparrow." Lady Agnes indicated a chair placed halfway down a long table set with chased silver and heavy crystal. Her use of Sparrow's Christian name betokened a certain informality, but her gestures and tone remained regal. Sparrow sat down meekly, hoping she would be able to get through the meal before the missing replacement arrived.

"There's your whiskey, girl." Sir Alasdair placed it before her and went to the head of the table, where he proceeded to carve a joint already placed there. Morag came in with a tureen of soup, went out, returned with a tray on which bowls of roast parsnips, mashed potatoes, carrots, and sprouts were set, and went out again.

Lady Agnes was ladling out the soup, ladling out four helpings, Sparrow noticed. There was a place laid opposite her, and for a moment she wondered if Morag was going to sit down with them, but as that unlikely supposition crossed her mind Lady Agnes nodded towards the empty place and said, "Someone hasn't heard the gong again."

"Mr. Roe is no slave to the beating of gongs," Sir Alasdair said, "but he will only have himself to blame if he comes to the table when the soup is cold."

Sparrow, tasting the fiery broth, decided that even when cold this soup would very probably sear the tongue.

"Curried, you know," Lady Agnes said, glancing at her expression. "Ever since he was out in India Sir Alasdair has enjoyed curried soup."

Sparrow, smiling manfully through the tears in her eyes, groped for the water glass and wondered how often the soup was served.

"Good Scottish mutton," Sir Alasdair boomed from the head of the table, "is one of the great pleasures of life. Eat up and put some flesh on your bones, child. Agnes, give the girl more mashed potato—ah! here is Mr. Roe."

The young gentleman entering the room had curling fair hair and unexpectedly dark eyes, the expression in them one of apology as he said, "I fear I am late again."

"We started the meal a few minutes early," Lady Agnes said mendaciously.

"Master Peter became extremely interested in the puzzle on which we were working," the young man said, taking his place opposite Sparrow.

"Peter usually becomes very engrossed in whatever he is doing as soon as his bedtime draws near," Lady Agnes said. "You must not allow him to bamboozle you, Mr. Roe."

"Had I known there was to be such a charming addition to the company I would have packed him off to his bed an hour ago," the other said, with a slight bow in Sparrow's direction.

"The replacement for Miss Marchmont," Lady Agnes supplied. "Miss Sparrow Harvey—foolish name, is it not?"

"To my ears it sounds charming," he said. "I trust that Miss Marchmont will not recover too rapidly."

"Mr. Charles Roe tutors my great-nephew," Lady Agnes said, ladling out soup. "Peter is eight and will soon be away to school but Mr. Roe is doing sterling work with him in the meantime."

Charles Roe gave another neat bow and proceeded to eat his soup with a caution that suggested he had tasted the fiery brew previously.

"Your nephew's son?" Sparrow hazarded.

Marie Sinclair had said that her fiancé was great-nephew to Sir Alasdair, but he must be more than eight years old. An elder brother to Peter, perhaps.

"My nephew, David's child," Sir Alasdair rumbled. "Clever little fellow. You shall meet him tomorrow, Miss Sparrow. And my wife is in error about your name. Suits you admirably. Mr. Roe, you will take some of the mutton? Our own sheep, you know."

"A slice or two only," Charles Roe replied. "Since I came to Craig Bothwell I have gained a considerable amount of weight."

He must have been very thin before then, Sparrow thought, glancing at his slender frame, the delicate bones of his face. It was a handsome face but there was something about the mouth that hinted at weakness. Then he turned long-lashed dark eyes in her direction and said in his light, melodious voice, "I hope that Lady Agnes can spare your company sometimes, Miss Harvey."

"Oh, do call her Sparrow," Lady Agnes said impatiently.

"I intend to do so. She is very pretty, don't you think?"

"Pretty enough to grace a throne," the tutor said, to which gallant compliment Sir Alasdair responded with a loud bellow of mirth, cut short by a knife-edged glare from his wife.

"We shall retire to the drawing-room for coffee and cake," that lady announced frostily.

"No pudding, ma'am?" Charles Roe asked playfully. "I so enjoy one of Mrs. Og's puddings."

"Apparently she ran out of suet," Lady Agnes said. "We shall endeavour to provide you with a pudding tomorrow, Mr. Roe. Sparrow, come and help me pour the coffee. It is a task that irritates me exceedingly since I can never recall how other people like their coffee to taste."

She rose, pushing back her chair, inclining her head to the gentlemen, who rose and swept out into the hall again and through a door on the right. Here a bright fire burned in the wide fireplace and long curtains of sleek bronze velvet shut out the evening. There were some excellent watercolours on the walls and the couches and chairs were piled with cushions in a manner that invited relaxation.

"You must try not to take Mr. Roe too seriously," Lady Agnes said, going over to a small table and beginning to slice a large cake. "He is a sad flirt."

"I thought his manner a trifle—familiar," Sparrow said.

"Educated in Germany," Lady Agnes said, as if that explained anything at all. "We are not accustomed to stand on ceremony here. You are from the south, of course. Now, was it cream or milk for Mr. Roe? I never can remember."

"Why not ask him when the gentlemen join us?" Sparrow suggested.

"His own memory is so excellent," Lady Agnes fretted, "that I like to—that must be one of your main considerations, my dear. I am inclined towards forgetfulness, which annoys my poor husband sadly. I shall be relying on you to keep me up to the mark. Cream. Yes, he definitely prefers cream. Looking at your complexion reminded me. Thank you kindly. We shall get on splendidly, I can see."

Somewhat bemused, Sparrow placed herself under the other's direction and, putting the fear of the genuine replacement's arrival to the back of her mind, poured coffee into cups of almost translucent delicacy.

"You see, Lady Agnes, we do not sit long after the ladies have deserted us." Charles Roe came in, his slight figure contrasting with that of his burly employer.

"Sit near to the fire," Lady Agnes instructed him. "You look cold, Mr. Roe."

"In Scotland the heart becomes so warm that the chilliness of one's limbs is of little account," he cried gaily. "Miss Sparrow, permit me to assist you. In these modern days it is for the gentlemen to serve."

"Yes, but—," Lady Agnes hesitated, then sat down abruptly, her skirts foaming about her.

"A dash of cream and a small teaspoon of sugar, I think?" Charles Roe glanced at Sparrow.

"Thank you." She relinquished her task and sat down herself.

"Tomorrow Master Peter and I shall walk down to the village and buy suet," he was continuing.

"My dear Mr. Roe, we would not dream—," Sir Alasdair began.

"Nonsense, sir, I shall thoroughly enjoy the expedition," he replied. "Perhaps Miss Sparrow will accompany us, if Lady Agnes can spare her?"

"I shall not require Sparrow until the afternoon tomorrow," Lady Agnes said.

"Then we shall set out after breakfast," Charles Roe said. "The countryside is so very fine round here, ma'am, that you must see it at its best."

Sparrow, accepting her coffee, sat in bewilderment. The tutor certainly had the Stuarts in the palm of his hand, she thought. Now he was seating himself in one of the most comfortable chairs.

"Sparrow's father has broken his leg," Lady Agnes proclaimed.

"That was Miss Marchmont, my dear," her husband informed her. "You are muddling things again."

"They both broke their legs," Lady Agnes said with dignity.

"Does your father know Miss Marchmont?" Sir Alasdair enquired.

"Not at all," Sparrow said truthfully.

"Have you seen her yourself since she had the accident?" This from Lady Agnes.

"Not to speak to," Sparrow said, hoping it was the right response.

Evidently it was since Lady Agnes exclaimed an instant later, "Of course, I was forgetting. Miss Marchmont informed me in her letter that she had written to a young acquaintance of hers to arrange for the young lady to fill in until she herself can travel."

"You have never met the good lady yourself?" Charles Roe asked.

"I got her through an advertisement in one of the English newspapers," Lady Agnes said. "I cannot approve of much in contemporary life but the advertisements are quite splendid. One can obtain all manner of things without stirring from one's chair. My dear, you are not eating your cake."

"I confess that I am a mite wearied after the journey," Sparrow said.

"The human body was not designed for sitting in stage-coaches," Sir Alasdair rumbled.

"You must feel free to retire," Lady Agnes seconded. "We eat our breakfast between eight and nine o'clock. Peter joins us then. We will see you in the morning."

"Thank you, Lady Agnes. Gentlemen." Sparrow rose with some relief.

"You will not forget that we are engaged to walk to the village in the morning?" Charles Roe reminded her, as she opened the door.

"No, I won't forget. Good night." Closing the door behind her, she resisted the temptation to put her ear to the wooden panels and went up the lamplit staircase.

The proposed walk to the village would afford her the opportunity of finding out how Lance was faring and also of posting a letter, since she assumed there would be either a post office or the means to send mail. Her father and Tizzie would be anxious to learn if she had reached her destination safely. The letter would go with the next stage, which, she calculated, would arrive on Saturday, continue up to Edinburgh, and begin the return on the Monday. By then the real replacement might well have arrived, but meanwhile it would do no harm to write.

In the gallery she slowed her step to look at the portraits, but the lights were too low for her to discern any details of features and all the portraits seemed to be of people clad in old-fashioned costume of the Elizabethan and Stuart periods.

She had almost reached the archway that gave onto the further passage when a soft footfall caused her to swing round nervously.

A small boy, clothed in nightshirt and dressing gown, stood at the far end of the gallery, watching her. As she paused, chiding herself for being so jumpy, he launched into a half-running, half-skipping step that brought him to her side.

"There was no pudding at supper," he said. "Did you get any pudding?"

"No, we didn't. Mrs. Og had run out of suet," Sparrow said.

"Mrs. Og is always running out of things," the child said. "She is almost as bad as Aunt Agnes."

"You are Peter?"

"Peter Stuart," he nodded with a quaint little bow. "Of course, she is my great-aunt, but that is altogether too much of a mouthful."

Whatever relationship he bore to Sir Alasdair and Lady Agnes, he wasn't Marie Sinclair's missing lover, Sparrow reasoned.

"We are to walk into the village with your tutor tomorrow morning to buy suet," she said aloud. "I am Sparrow Harvey."

"You've come instead of Miss Marchmont," he said. "Aunt Agnes told me that she had broken her leg. Uncle Alasdair was pleased about that."

"Oh, surely not!" Sparrow cried.

"She was engaged to come several months ago," Peter explained, "after she had worked out her notice in her previous position, but Uncle Alasdair wished to write and tell her not to come. He has taken a dislike to strangers."

"He was very cordial to me," Sparrow objected.

"Perhaps he changed his mind," Peter said, shrugging. "You don't look old enough to be a companion."

"And you are certainly not old enough to make personal remarks," she chided.

"Nor to stay up for dinner nor to use a gun nor to ask questions," he sighed. "But nobody has informed me that I am not old enough to learn lessons or to be told to hold my tongue."

"You do not look as if you often hold your tongue," Sparrow said consideringly.

The little boy gave a crow of laughter and looked suddenly like his great-aunt.

"I like talking," he said simply. "There are not many children of my own age hereabouts so I practise on the adults. You are from London?"

"And this is the first time I was in Scotland. Shouldn't you be in your bed? Your tutor—"

"Oh, I never take any notice of tutors." The childish lip curled. "They are all too anxious to keep their place to be very harsh with me. My great-aunt and uncle would not allow me to be ill treated, you know. I am the last hope of the House of Stuart."

"Are you indeed?" Sparrow hesitated, then risked, "What of your brother?"

"I haven't got a brother," Peter said. "My mama died when I was born, and my papa died when I was two. That is very sad, is it not?"

Adam Stuart must derive from another branch of the family then, Sparrow reckoned.

"Very sad," she said, somewhat belatedly. "However, you have a happy home here, don't you?"

"It will be mine one day so I had better be happy here," he said with another crow of laughter. "Did you know the room where you are sleeping was once slept in by Mary Stuart? She was the queen of Scotland, you know, and very sad and beautiful."

"She must have been very clever too," Sparrow observed, "to sleep in a house that wasn't built until more than a hundred years after her death."

"Are you a governess?" Peter asked, looking impressed.

"No, but I liked history when I was at school."

"Would you be frightened if there were ghosts here?" he wanted to know.

"Not in the least," Sparrow said firmly, "because I don't believe in them anyway. Now you had better go to your own bed, hadn't you? Poor Mr. Roe may get into trouble if you are discovered wandering about."

"Not he," Peter said. "Why, he comes and goes as he pleases, you know. I am rather a spoilt child but he is a very spoilt tutor. Good-night, Miss Sparrow." He turned on his heel and sped down the length of the gallery, leaving Sparrow to gaze after him thoughtfully.

If he was Sir Alasdair's great-nephew and bore the same surname, then his grandfather must have been brother to Sir Alasdair, and Adam Stuart must descend from another brother, possibly a younger one since it was Peter to whom the house would belong one day. She would have to make further enquiry in the morning.

Morag had evidently found the time to light the lamps in her room and pass a warming pan over the turned-down sheets. The curtains had been drawn close and the chamber had a welcoming air. Sparrow wondered briefly how long she would be able to occupy it before the real companion arrived, and decided that worrying about it would do no good at all. With any luck she would find out what she wanted to know and have manufactured an excuse to leave before she was discovered. Certainly there was nothing here to justify Marie Sinclair's trepidation. Whatever the young man's reasons for disappearing, the house and its occupants were far from sinister, though Lady Agnes might be termed eccentric.

She had brought paper and pen and was pleased to find a full inkwell on the window ledge. Seating herself by the window and looping back one curtain slightly she began writing, pausing now and then to think of phrases that could be read by both her father and Tizzie.

> Dear Papa and Tizzie,
>
> This is to reassure you that I travelled here safely though I am still wearied after the long journey. I had a peaceful night at York but was disappointed that it was too dark when we arrived for me to see anything of the city.
> The house here is large and handsome and I was greeted with every consideration. I look forward to the companionship I shall share here."

Would Tizzie be sharp enough to pick up on that word? Sparrow hoped so. She dipped her pen in the ink again and wrote on.

> "Not that I am grumbling about your company, but a change is as good as a rest, they say. The garden here is very fine and from the little I have seen of the surrounding countryside I shall enjoy some good walks."

She had better temper her enthusiasm lest she find herself on the way south again within a few days. She ended somewhat hastily,

> But I do confess that already I am feeling nasty little

pangs of homesickness, so I have not yet set any definite time for my return.

Your Loving,

Sparrow

The letter would have to be franked for her. She would ask Sir Alasdair if he would be so kind. She looked about for sealing wax, and discovered a piece near the inkwell. Both were unusual to find in a bedroom. Holding the wax close to the red coals burning in the grate, folding and sealing the missive, and writing her father's name and address, she wondered if the room had once been a schoolroom, and had been converted at some recent date for the expected companion. A closer examination convinced her that she had hit upon the truth. The carpet and curtains were new and bright, but there were some slightly battered books on the shelf by the bed and a box containing chalk in the top drawer of the tallboy.

The books were various volumes on geographical and natural history subjects. She pulled one out, opened it, and read the straggling words across the flyleaf:

"This book belongs to Adam Stuart, aged seven years and five months. 1791."

So Adam Stuart did exist and had once conned his lessons in this room. Sparrow put the book back on the shelf with a feeling of relief. All she needed to do now was to find him.

= 6 =

IN THE MORNING Morag came with hot water, a cup of coffee, and the information that it was a fine, bright day for a walk.

Sparrow chose to put on a simple woollen gown in a faint chequered pattern of brown and white. Her hair was too short to coil into a decorous chignon, and no amount of combing would coax her rebellious curls to straighten. She threaded a brown ribbon through the auburn mass, attached her reticule to her wrist by its short strap, drank her cooling coffee, and went briskly along the passage.

"Good morning, I was waiting for you to wake up."

Peter was in the gallery beyond, nightclothes now exchanged for breeches and a high-necked fisherman's jersey. In the pale sunlight streaming through the windows he was revealed as a slight child who looked as if he would grow into a tall adult, his hair and eyes midway between brown and dark blond. Hazel was the word she would have used to describe him, and there was something vital and springlike in his alert stance and inquisitive gaze that reminded her of a young sapling that might grow straight or be twisted by the wind.

"Are you going to escort me down to breakfast?" she asked, smiling.

"I had mine hours ago in the kitchen with Morag," he informed her. "It is more agreeable to hear Morag talking than to hear Uncle Alasdair telling us all that the country is going to the devil."

Sparrow attempted a frown but found the corners of her mouth wrinkling into a grin. "I must go and eat my own breakfast quickly then," she said hastily. "We are to walk to the village, are we not?"

"Mr. Roe and I will wait for you," Peter said and sped off as if his legs had no patience with standing still.

Continuing down the staircase and turning towards the dining-room Sparrow was intercepted by Lady Agnes, powdered and panniered as she had been the previous day.

"Oh, not the main dining-room, dear," that lady said. "Far too draughty early in the morning. We eat breakfast and luncheon in the solar—Sir Alasdair calls it the Nookery, since he will have no truck with medievalism. We have almost finished, but Morag will bring hot toast. This is the day Jessie and Florrie come over to clean the place. We do not keep many indoor servants, you know. One falls over them rather."

"I have written to my father to let him know that I arrived safely," Sparrow said, turning obediently in the direction the other indicated, "and I hoped Sir Alasdair would frank it for me."

"Yes, of course he will. Sir Alasdair is always obliging except when he is in a temper," Lady Agnes said cheerfully. "This morning he is in quite a pleasant humour. Have you met Peter?"

"He's a nice child."

"A very nice child." The older woman's sternly patrician features softened. "Very clever for his age, you know. Very intelligent. He will do well at school, though we shall miss him—I was just saying that we shall miss Peter when he goes to school, won't we, dear?"

They had ended up in a small room with breakfast laid on a round table and the morning sunlight competing with the flames dancing in the hearth.

"I heard what you were saying," Sir Alasdair said testily. "Not deaf, you know. Good morning, Missy. You look very bright and fresh. Going into the village to buy suet, aren't you? I don't wish to miss my pudding again."

"I can get whatever is needed while I'm there," Sparrow said helpfully. "I have written to my father and I was hoping that—"

"I'll frank it for you." He had an irritating habit of finishing off sentences for one as if he were too impatient to listen any longer, but she handed over the letter gratefully.

"The mushrooms are very good," Lady Agnes said, lifting the cover from a silver tureen, "but the kidneys look a mite peculiar. You will take porridge?"

"I am not fond of porridge," Sparrow confessed, taking a seat at the table.

"Not fond of porridge?" Lady Agnes echoed. "Why, I never heard of—Alasdair, did you hear?"

"Tried not to," he said gruffly, returning with the franked letter and handing it to her. "No wonder she's such a little scrap of a thing, Agnes. No stamina. Now I've had a bowl of salted oatmeal and milk every morning of my life—"

"Not on the first few mornings of your life, dear," Lady Agnes broke in. "You would not have been able to digest it, you know."

"Don't pick me up on every word," Sir Alasdair said. "The oatmeal here could be given to newborn babies with no harm whatsoever to their digestions."

Under cover of the altercation Sparrow helped herself surreptitiously to bacon and tomatoes.

"Possibly without salt," Sir Alasdair was saying. "That I will grant you, but Mr. Roe himself complimented the cook on the quality of the porridge here, and one assumes he has an epicurean taste. Where was I?"

"About to go through the rent roll, dear," his wife said.

"So I was. Thank you. Enjoy your walk, my dear." He stomped out, taking much of the vitality in the room with him.

"Was there anything else you wanted in the village, Lady Agnes?" Sparrow thought it politic to ask. "You have not yet outlined my duties."

"Oh, just be on hand when I need you," Lady Agnes said vaguely. "I am apt to forget things, and sometimes Alasdair is busy elsewhere and hasn't time to remind me. This afternoon we must make out the invitations."

"For what?" Sparrow enquired.

"For the celebrations marking Sir Alasdair's seventy-fifth birthday, of course. Three-quarters of a century is an immense span to have lived, you know."

"I suppose it is," Sparrow said, adding cautiously, "You will be much younger than your husband then."

"Only six years," Lady Agnes said. "Ladies wear better than gentlemen though, live longer too. We are to have quite a lively time of it, I assure you. More than a hundred from all over Scotland are coming, not to mention a few from over the border."

"When is the party to be?" Sparrow enquired.

"A week on Monday," Lady Agnes informed her.

"But there will not be time to send them out and receive replies."

"Oh, everybody has known for ages there are to be celebrations," Lady Agnes said. "It is only a matter of confirming the time. Now you had better make haste. One wouldn't wish to keep Mr. Roe waiting."

Sparrow couldn't quite see why not, but she rose obediently and went through to the hall, where a girl with her head tied up in a scarf was polishing the woodwork. Through the open door Sparrow could see the tutor standing, patiently waiting, while his pupil ran round and round on the lawn.

"Good morning, Miss Sparrow." Mr. Roe essayed a slight bow as she came down the steps. "Will you not require a pelisse? The wind can be quite chilly."

"I am just going to get my pelisse and bonnet," Sparrow explained, "but I came to ask you to wait a few moments more, if you don't object?"

"Oh, please don't hurry on my account," he returned instantly. "I am well used to waiting. Yes, very well accustomed to delay."

For some reason the sentence seemed to amuse him. His dark eyes glinted with laughter, and then a brief shadow fell across his mobile features and he sighed deeply.

"A moment only," Sparrow promised and flew back upstairs. Her pelisse and straw bonnet were quickly donned and she hurried down again.

"You look charming, Miss Sparrow—if you will excuse my addressing you by your Christian name?" Charles Roe said as they set off down the drive with Peter scampering head. "It is an unusual name."

"I believe so," Sparrow said demurely. She had confided the reason for the name to Simon Adair, but she felt no compulsion to confide in Charles Roe, though he was being both friendly and polite.

"And you are from London? Scotland seems a considerable distance to travel to obtain a post."

"I am here only temporarily," she said, wondering how temporary she was going to be.

"Instead of the unfortunate Miss Marchmont. Sir Alasdair mentioned that your father has also suffered an accident recently."

"A riding accident," Sparrow said. "Oh, but the view is lovely."

They had gone through a side gate onto a bridle path that opened out onto a sloping expanse of grass starred with wildflowers with a cobbled path leading down to a cluster of houses in the shallow valley below.

"That is Craigsmuir," Peter said, running back to them. "The lands here used to belong to the Earls of Bothwell in the olden times. Now Bothwell must have slept in the village, don't you think, Miss Sparrow?"

"Very probably," Sparrow said and laughed.

"What was that about?" Charles Roe wanted to know.

"Oh, Peter was trying to frighten me last night with a tale of Mary, Queen of Scots having slept in my bedroom, more than a century before the house was built," Sparrow told him.

"Her Grace may well have spent a night in the old keep," he said. "That is fourteenth century, I am told."

"It looks rather a grim place."

"I believe it is unsafe," he said. "Even castles crumble if they are not looked after. Only bats nest there now."

"In that case I shall certainly avoid it," Sparrow said firmly. "I know one is supposed to love all dumb creatures but I never could find any affection in my heart for bats."

He laughed, touching her arm lightly as they stepped onto the cobbles. "I trust you have sturdy shoes," he warned. "Hereabouts many still run about barefoot, not because they cannot afford shoes but because some of the paths are precipitous and one needs to get a good grip on the stone."

"You were brought up in Germany, Lady Agnes said?" Sparrow ventured.

"Since boyhood. Have you ever visited there?"

"This is the first time I was ever out of England."

"Then we must teach you to love Scotland. It is God's own country, you know," he said, taking her arm again as they forded a shallow stream and entered the village proper.

Unlike an English village where the houses usually meandered along the street towards the village green with its maypole and stocks, this village had its cottages erected in a semicircle with the green in the centre and at some distance the long, low bulk of a kirk with a graveyard at the side enclosed within a stone wall.

"For protection," Charles Roe said, interpreting her look of curiosity. "There were often raids between neighbouring clans in the old days and so people tended to huddle close for protection. On the first day of the new year the last of the bannocks baked the previous year were rolled down the hill towards the Beltane fires and depending on what happened to the bannock one's fortune during the year ahead could be foretold."

"You know a lot about the local customs," Sparrow said.

"I familiarised myself with the district," he replied. "A tutor ought to have some knowledge, don't you think?"

His dark eyes were mocking her again. She wondered why and moved slightly away, saying in brisk, businesslike tones, "Lady Agnes did not provide me with any money with which to buy the suet, and I neglected to ask the quantity. What are we to do?"

"I have both the quantity required and the money needed tucked away in my head and my pocket respectively," he said lightly. "Why don't you leave the tedium of purchasing to me and explore the village? The kirk is Saxon, they tell me. We can meet here in an hour." An hour was a generous allowance. Sparrow reckoned that ten minutes would exhaust the possibilities of exploration. On the other hand she wanted to post her letter and also to discover if Lance had succeeded in finding shelter.

Peter had already run towards one of the thatched cottages, calling in his piping treble, "Mrs. MacGregor, we are come to buy suet, if you please."

"Master Peter, no need to bellow to wake the dead," the person addressed remonstrated, putting down the trowel with which she was digging in a small patch of cabbages. "I told Morag his lordship would be in a miff not to be having his pudding, but there—would the lass be wanting anything?"

Her eyes, black currants in the rosy expanse of her face, moved to Sparrow.

"To post a letter," Sparrow said.

"Give it to me and I'll see that Tom gets it. He rides with the post and catches up with the stage. Where would the letter be for?"

"For London," Sparrow said, taking it from her reticule.

"He'll need to be catching up with the return stage then," Mrs. MacGregor said. "You'll be the lass come to help out with the party."

"Allow me to present Miss Harvey," Charles Roe said with a slight flourish. That flourish was wasted on the good lady, who merely nodded and went into the cottage, saying over her shoulder, "If you want suet, then you must come and help me weigh it. I've no help today. Master Peter, there are some sweetmeats ready-made and you may have some if your tutor agrees."

"An hour then," Sparrow said, feeling rather at a loss as her companions left her. She turned and made her way slowly past the semicircle of houses, noting that all were trim and in good repair. Sir Alasdair was obviously a good landlord, if he were the landlord. There had been a sturdy independence in the woman's manner that suggested the people hereabouts might own their own homes.

She had expected the Scots to be a hospitable nation, but though several people were walking across the turf or standing by their gates nobody responded to her smile. Clearly, she had been romanticising again. She could imagine Simon Adair's drawling, "Clannish is the word. And not overfond of the Sassenachs, my dear Sparrow."

She frowned, irritated with herself for having let him enter her mind again. It was in the highest degree unlikely that she would have anything further to do with him, but at that moment she would have welcomed his company.

There being nothing to see in the village she turned her steps towards the kirk. The large graveyard would surely contain some Stuarts and give her a clearer idea of the family of which Marie Sinclair's sweetheart was a member.

So far Adam's name had not even been mentioned. She wished she had asked Marie for a full description of the missing man, but the whole encounter had been so unexpected and happened so rapidly that she had not had her wits about her.

The kirk was set on a rise and seemed to brood over the houses below. She paused at the lych-gate and looked down to where the high banks of gorse led to the larger Craig Bothwell.

The landscape was certainly beautiful but even in sunshine there was a rugged grandeur about it. No parading tulips here but gorse and whinberry and further down the valley the dark sheen of bluebells. A man might vanish here and not be found again, she thought, and found that she was shivering.

She pressed down the latch of the gate and went in,

walking between the granite and marble headstones with a somewhat lagging step.

"Miss Sparrow. Hey!"

She recognised the voice before she turned her head to see Lancelot Higgindrop seated on the edge of a tablelike tomb, looking like a grimy elf.

"I wondered if you were all right," Sparrow said, walking back to greet him. "Did you find a bed for the night? There doesn't seem to be an inn here."

"And if there was I wouldn't be spending good money in it," he said decidedly. "I found myself a job—sleep in the barn, rake grass, pull the cart, dig turnips, for one shilling a week and as much to eat as you like."

"Who is employing you?" she enquired.

"The Widow Mackintosh—they 'ave some queer names roundabout," he said. "The rest of 'em reckon she's a witch because she lives alone with a cat, but she seems all right to me. Course, I didn't mention as 'ow you and me is friends."

"Perhaps you will like it well enough to settle down here," Sparrow said.

"Not me, Miss." He shook his head. "I'm 'ere to see you get 'ome safe when you feels like going. And you ain't no kitchen skivvy neither from the looks of you, or are you really staying with friends?"

"I am filling in for a Miss Marchmont, who is coming here in a few weeks to be a companion to Lady Agnes Stuart," Sparrow told him.

"Are they treating you decent?" he asked earnestly.

"Yes," said Sparrow, touched by his concern. "Yes, they are treating me very decently."

"Because if they ain't then you just let me know," her cavalier said threateningly.

"I came to look round the churchyard," Sparrow said. "I wanted to check up on the Stuarts here. I wonder where their family tombs would be."

Looking about as she spoke she answered her own

question an instant later as she caught sight of a railed enclosure at a little distance.

"That must be it. It's the most conspicuous monument in the graveyard."

"You don't 'alf use long words," Lance complained, trotting after her.

"I meant that as the Stuarts are the most important family here, as far as I know, then it stands to reason that they would have the grandest tomb. Well, at least the gate is unlocked."

"Even if it wasn't we could shin over the wall," Lance said, doing so.

"I prefer to use the gate," Sparrow said with unwonted primness. "Oh, but it looks like a little house."

"With an angel on top," Lance said, squinting up at the stone figure. "Does he 'ave that sword to stop 'em from getting out?"

"Don't be so foolish," Sparrow said coldly, pushing away the image his words conjured up.

"Do they pile 'em in one on top of t'other?" he pursued, unsnubbed.

"I suppose there will be shelves inside." She looked with some dismay at the names and dates engraved on the stone slab that served to seal the entrance. A step to either side showed more names. The Stuarts obviously believed in keeping together.

"They have to be in chronological order, I suppose." She went round to the back of the tomb and saw that only the top half of the stone was engraved.

"Room for more here," Lance said cheerfully.

"So I see." Sparrow tried to emulate his own unimaginative unconcern. After all, it was a bright, sunny morning, and there was no reason to feel any sense of creeping unease.

"What names was you looking for?" Lance enquired. "Not that I can 'elp. Not too 'ot in the reading department."

"I'm not sure." She stooped slightly, running her eye down the list. Alasdair seemed a popular name in the family. An Alasdair Stuart had fallen at Flodden, another at Stirling. There were several Davids and Peters too, and an Adam.

Adam Stuart, born 1723 and died at Culloden in 1745.

She murmured the words aloud and saw Lance giving her an enquiring look.

"What was Culloden?" he asked.

"The last battle of the 'Forty-Five Rebellion," she said.

"What's that when it's at 'ome?" he demanded.

Sparrow stifled a sigh, trying to think of a way to encapsulate several history lessons in one brief explanation.

"The Stuart kings used to rule England and Scotland," she said at last.

"The Stuarts that live 'ere?" Lance looked impressed.

"No, of course not. These others were royal Stuarts. Anyway, the English sent the last Stuart king away and got themselves another king, which the Scots didn't like very much."

"I'm not surprised if they wasn't asked," Lance said.

"The Stuart kings tried to come back and take the throne again. The last time was in seventeen forty-five but there was a battle at a place called Culloden and the rebellion failed. Bonnie Prince Charlie escaped to France and never tried again."

"Do you think that he might?"

"It's not very likely," Sparrow said discouragingly. "He'd be nearly a hundred years old if he was alive, which he is not. But this Adam Stuart obviously supported him and fell at Culloden. Isn't that interesting?"

"Not really," Lance said flatly. "It's all 'istory, ain't it?"

"I suppose so." Sparrow sighed briefly again, thinking that the romance of the past was wasted on ignorant mudlarks.

"There's another A-D-A-M down 'ere," Lance said, tracing each letter with his forefinger. It was next to the last name on the list.

"Adam Stuart, born seventeen eighty-four. Died eighteen hundred," read Sparrow aloud.

Below that was engraved, "Phyllida Stuart, born seventeen eighty, died eighteen hundred and three."

"If there were some clue as to who was related to whom it would help," Sparrow said crossly.

There was no reply. Looking up, she beheld Lance dashing away between the other tombstones, while from the other direction a black-garbed figure was approaching.

"Good morning to you, Miss—?" The minister paused at the wall and gave her a searching look from beneath heavy white brows.

"Harvey," she supplied. "I have come as a temporary companion to Lady Agnes."

"Ah, yes, she did mention it." He nodded. "I hope the lad was not fretting you? I told Fay Mackintosh that she ought not to go taking waifs and strays into her employ but she's a woman with a mind of her own. You are exploring the Stuarts?"

"Just exploring," she evaded. "They're an old family. Jacobites?"

"Find me a Stuart anywhere in Scotland who was not," he returned gloomily. "That was an ill-starred family, Miss Harvey, that brought great misery to many good people."

"I was looking at the more recent names," Sparrow said. "Adam Stuart, died in eighteen hundred?"

"That was a sad affair." He shook his head. "Sir Alasdair's great-nephew. A shooting incident. One warns boys to take care but they forget. He tripped in the heather and the gun he was carrying went off. It killed him instantly, and the shock and sorrow killed his mother too. Poor Fiona was laid beside him before the year was out. His father, David, was distraught. I never saw a man so hard hit."

"I was wondering where Peter fitted in," Sparrow said. "One doesn't like to pry."

"And the subject is still painful. Peter is the grandson of Sir Alasdair's elder brother, Adam. He fell at Culloden."

"I was just looking at that," Sparrow pointed.

"There was a considerable difference in age between the brothers," the minister said. "Sir Alasdair—who was not

97

then Sir Alasdair, of course—would have been about three while Adam was in his early twenties. Adam's death meant that he became the laird, of course."

"His brother was married?"

"To a local lass, Fiona Argyll. Their son, David, was born only weeks after his father's death."

"Then wasn't he the heir?"

"The estate has an entail," the minister explained. "It passes from brother to brother in the same generation, in each generation, as a matter of fact. David would have inherited after his uncle."

"And David is—was Peter's father?"

She felt uneasy about asking so many questions, but the minister seemed pleased to show off his local knowledge to a stranger.

"Adam's and Peter's," he said. "By different mothers. After Adam was accidentally killed and Fiona died David took a second wife, Phyllida MacHale, who died giving birth to Peter. David was killed at Trafalgar, which is why he doesn't lie here with his ancestors. There is a table to his memory within the kirk."

"So father and son both married a Fiona?"

"Adam married Fiona Argyll and his son, David, married first a Fiona Macpherson. The name is a popular one in the Highlands."

"Is Adam a popular name too?"

"Not as popular, though there are Adams in various families, of course. David named his elder son after his own father, of course. He was always proud of the fact that the older Adam had died fighting for the Cause."

"Peter said he didn't have any brothers," Sparrow said.

"In literal terms he doesn't. Adam was his half brother, and Peter never knew him or his mother."

"And Sir Alasdair and Lady Agnes have no children?"

"A great sorrow," the minister said, shaking his head. "They adored their nephew, David, and his son, Adam, was the apple of their eye. Then Adam died and Peter was born and David was killed at Trafalgar and now they look upon little Peter as their own. Apt to indulge him, though he's a nice little lad."

"Wasn't David Stuart a bit elderly to be fighting at Trafalgar?" Sparrow asked, doing quick sums in her head.

"He was only sixty." The minister looked slightly put out. "Men often reach their peak if they survive into their fifties and sixties. Peter was only two then, of course. He cannot remember either of his parents but his great-uncle and aunt have amply supplied their lack."

"No Adam Stuarts left alive then," Sparrow said.

"Not in Sir Alasdair's family."

"Well, it's very interesting," she said, carefully casual, "and I will know which topics of conversation to avoid. One doesn't want to give pain by mentioning something inadvertently. Thank you for giving me your time, Mr.—?"

"I fear I left my good manners in yesterday's cassock," he said apologetically. "James Laurie, minister of this parish— Scottish Reformed Kirk. I hope we will see you at service tomorrow?"

"Oh, I shall look forward to it," Sparrow assured him. She would have liked to take another look at the lists of names, to fix them in her mind, but the minister clearly expected her to leave. She took a fleeting glance at the huge mausoleum with its guarding angel and turned back towards the gate.

There was no sign of Lance as she walked slowly. Well, at least he had landed on his feet.

What she now had to consider was what to do next. If the last Adam Stuart had tripped and shot himself eleven years before, then the man for whom Marie Sinclair was looking had to be an impostor—unless Adam Stuart hadn't really died. Perhaps there had been some mystery about the accident and he'd merely pretended to be dead. Sparrow couldn't imagine why such a course of action would have been pursued. However if Adam Stuart was, by some freak chance, still alive, then that made him the heir to Craig

Bothwell and not his younger half brother, Peter. And if, on the other hand, Adam Stuart had really been killed, then someone might be pretending to be him. Which could mean that Peter was in some kind of danger.

Sparrow let herself out through the lych-gate, and began lecturing herself severely on her overheated imagination as she went. It was a mistake to weave mysteries where there were probably none at all and Marie Sinclair had merely been cozened by a rogue.

Peter and his tutor were waiting for her. She put a smile on her face and went to meet them.

= 7 =

"DID YOU HAVE an interesting walk round, Miss Sparrow?" Charles Roe enquired.

"Very interesting, thank you." She gave him a bland smile. "Graveyards are so full of history."

"Graveyards," Peter announced, "are full of skeletons."

"I suppose they are," Sparrow admitted with a chuckle. "I see you have the suet."

"So Uncle Alasdair will get his pudding," Peter said. "Mrs. Og makes splendid puddings."

"And your letter was handed over to Tom," Charles Roe said, "so we can enjoy the walk back. You know I am falling in love with Scotland."

"It's a beautiful country," Sparrow agreed, "but the people don't seem very friendly."

"They are shy with strangers," the tutor informed her, "but once they trust you then there are no finer friends on earth. There's to be a grand gathering of all the neighbours to mark Sir Alasdair's birthday."

"For which I promised Lady Agnes to write out the invitations." Sparrow hastened her footsteps guiltily. "I must contrive to earn my salary." If I am able to remain undetected for sufficiently long enough to collect anything, her thoughts added silently.

"There is no need to hurry," Charles Roe assured her. "Sir Alasdair and Lady Agnes do not time the comings and goings of those who work for them. They are most congenial employers."

"They appear to appreciate you immensely," Sparrow said. "I never had a tutor myself but I am sure few of them receive much consideration."

"Oh, I have no complaints." Charles Roe flashed her a smile. It lifted the somewhat sad lines into which his expression settled when he was not actually talking. He was, she reckoned, about seven or eight and twenty, but there were moments when he seemed older.

"You have known less amiable treatment, I suppose?" she said.

"As a tutor? Oh, I am new to the profession," he told her. "Originally I was trained as a soldier, but a bad bout of fever forced me to resign my commission, and I turned to the field of education. It is less dangerous than war but often fully as wearisome."

"That is not very complimentary to your pupil, sir."

"On the contrary," he returned, "it is a sincere compliment since this young gentleman is forward for his age and keeps me on my toes."

Sparrow smiled and they walked on together, Peter covering twice the distance since he kept running backwards and forwards, pointing out a birds' nest high in an ash tree, chanting the riddles beloved by children of his age.

There was no sign of Lady Agnes when they reached Craig Bothwell though a pervading smell of polish told them the cleaning was still going on. Leaving Charles Roe and Peter to deliver the suet to the kitchen, Sparrow went up to her room. It was still short of noon, which gave her a little time. She took paper and pen and sat down by the wide windowsill to clarify the information she had gleaned from the minister.

"Adam Stuart and Sir Alasdair were brothers with a wide gap of years between their ages. Adam married a Fiona and was killed at Culloden, leaving David, who was his son. David married another Fiona and had a son, Adam. Adam accidentally shot himself when he was sixteen and his mother died soon afterwards. Then David took a second wife, Phyllida, who died when Peter was born, and David himself was killed at Trafalgar soon afterwards."

She looked thoughtfully at what she had written. It was fairly straightforward but there was still someone calling himself Adam Stuart, great-nephew of Sir Alasdair, walking round and paying court to Marie Sinclair. Then he had come up to see his great-uncle and never come back. Marie Sinclair had said she had written to him every week but there had been no replies and none of her letters had been returned. One had to work, therefore, on the assumption that Adam Stuart, whoever he was, had come to Craig Bothwell where either he had simply decided to ignore the letters—or some harm had befallen him.

At this point in her cogitations Sparrow tore up her notes and fed them to the flames dancing on the hearth. Craig Bothwell and its occupants, despite the sadness of the family history and the romanticism of its setting, were as far from sinister as it was possible to be.

She took off her outer garments, tried vainly to flatten down her springing curls, and went down to the room that Lady Agnes had titled the solar, and Sir Alasdair, the Nookery. A cold collation was laid out on the round table. The glazed ham, the bright salad, the poached salmon in its coat of aspic awakened her appetite. She was debating whether or not to begin when Morag entered, bearing a large pot of coffee.

"Sir Alasdair went over to take a bite with the reeve," she volunteered, "and Lady Agnes went for a wee lie-down. Is coffee fine for you or do you prefer tea?"

"Coffee is fine. It smells delicious," Sparrow said, taking a seat.

"Mother's mixing a pudding at this minute, with Mr. Roe and Master Peter teasing her to let them have a stir. Would there be anything else you might need?"

"Nothing, thank you. You look after us all splendidly," Sparrow said.

"The Stuarts are like family," Morag said. "I was born in this house and my parents were married in it."

"Then you will remember Adam, Peter's half-brother?"

The cheerful smile on Morag's face faded. "Very well," she said. "He and I were the same age. We used to play together, do our lessons together sometimes. Sir Alasdair wanted him to be brought up here since it would be his own one day."

"That was a terrible accident," Sparrow said.

"Yes, it was terrible." Morag hesitated, then went on, "They don't talk about Adam now. The subject is too painful, you understand?"

"Even after eleven years?" Sparrow persisted.

"It was the first of them—the deaths, I mean." Morag had lowered her voice slightly and her high-coloured complexion was paler, the freckles standing out on her nose. "Adam first and then a few weeks later Mistress Fiona just faded away, and then Mr. David went off and came back with a new wife from Edinburgh. A bit of a lass she was, but very sweet, and she had Master Peter and died of it and Mr. David went back to sea and died at Trafalgar. A real run of ill luck it was, and there were some in the village said that someone must be wishing us ill, but I reckon it was chance. Since then everything has been quiet and peaceful. Now, if you'll pardon me, I have to get back to the kitchen."

She strode out, closing the door behind her.

Sparrow helped herself to salmon and ate it without appreciating the delicate flavour. There was certainly no doubt in anyone's mind that Adam Stuart was dead. The man who had told Marie Sinclair that he was Adam Stuart had been an impostor then. Yet he had not chosen a name at random since there had been a real great-nephew of Sir Alasdair's called Adam. He had not, however, been aware of all the family business, since he had told Marie that his great-uncle had always promised to remember him in his will, and the minister had talked of an entail by which Adam would have inherited after his father's death anyway.

Sparrow finished her luncheon and decided that her best course of action was to write to Marie Sinclair, telling Marie what she had discovered and suggesting that she make arrangements to leave Craig Bothwell. The real replacement would soon arrive. Sparrow hoped to be gone before then. Quite apart from the difficulty of giving any explanation, she was beginning to feel uncomfortably like an impostor herself.

Lady Agnes was just emerging from her own room when Sparrow entered the corridor. She was clad, as usual, in the full-skirted dress and had hair powdered in the style of thirty years before. The effect made her look as if she were trapped in time, Sparrow mused, but her tone was entirely matter-of-fact as she said, "Ah, my dear, there you are. I have the guest list here. It is simply a matter of filling in the names on the invitation cards and the correct addresses. I cannot recall half of the people we have asked to come. It will be a large gathering, with a bonfire and fireworks, and plenty of whiskey for the guests. You have a suitable dress?"

"I have an evening gown," Sparrow hesitated, inwardly blessing Tizzie, "but it isn't like your style of dressing."

"Nobody dresses as I do any longer," Lady Agnes said with a small sigh as she led the way back into her bedchamber, a large handsomely furnished room with tapestry hung against the walls and an immense tester bed. "Such femininity is out of style these days. Skirts like tubes and hair the colour Nature decided it. No subtlety. However, I am in a minority. Here is the list, my dear. Feel free to take your time over it. You may take the invitations as you choose—alphabetically, perhaps?"

"Thank you, Lady Agnes."

Sparrow seated herself at the large flat-topped desk in the window and hoped that her employer wouldn't hover over her. Fortunately, after fluttering around Sparrow for a few moments, Lady Agnes murmured something indeterminate and swept out, her skirts hissing over the carpet.

Sparrow bent her attention to the list, noting that most names seemed to begin with "Mac". The addresses were scrawled at the side in a spiky hand that was obviously that of Lady Agnes, who would, no doubt, object to using a clear, modern hand. The invitation cards were in a neat pile at the side. Engraved inside the cards was the legend,

> Sir Alasdair and Lady Agnes Stuart
> of Craig Bothwell have pleasure in inviting
>
> to a Celebration in honour of Sir Alasdair's
> seventy-fifth birthday."

A date nine days hence and the time of eight P.M. were in the lower right-hand corner. There was also a pile of envelopes already franked. Working her way through the list Sparrow wondered where the guests were all going to be accommodated, since many of them lived in remote corners of the country. Perhaps they were to be lodged in the village or perhaps the party went on all night.

The afternoon wore on. The house was silent. One forgot, she thought, that the walls were of thick stone so that sounds were muffled between one room and the next. Now and then she raised her head, listening to the absence of traffic noises beyond the windows. In London she scarcely heard the rattling of wheels and clip-clopping of hooves, but here the peace was almost absolute. She wondered if Peter was occupied now with his lessons. In such a big house the presence of a child made little difference.

The last card written and addressed, she stretched and flexed the aching muscles of her back. There was paper on the desk. She took a sheet and wrote rapidly,

> Dear Miss Sinclair,
> The great-nephew of Sir Alasdair Stuart was killed in a shooting accident eleven years ago when he was a boy of sixteen. There seems no doubt about this, and there is no other Adam Stuart connected with the family or in the neighbourhood save his grandfather, who was killed at Culloden. The only gentleman of the approximately right age here is Mr. Roe, the tutor, but as you gave me no physical description of Mr. Stuart it is difficult

for me to make enquiry. Please write to me by return
if you have fresh instructions,

> I remain,
> S. Harvey.

As she penned the address she reflected there was no point
in explaining that she too was here under false pretences and
might be dismissed at any time. Marie Sinclair had struck her
as a singularly unresourceful young woman who panicked and
had very little sense of adventure.

"Finished already?" Lady Agnes had returned, her face
wreathed in a pleased smile. "What an excellent secretary
you do make, my dear. Now all that's left to do is take them
down to the village, and when Tom rides out he may take
them all with him."

"If you don't require me for anything else I can walk down
to the village now," Sparrow offered.

Marie Sinclair's weekly letters had not been returned to
her. It might be wiser not to reveal the fact that she was
writing to a Miss Sinclair.

"There is nothing whatsoever to do until dinner," Lady
Agnes said amiably. "You are sure the walk will not fatigue
you? Morag can always—"

"I enjoy exercise," Sparrow said. "In London it is considered slightly eccentric of me, but then there are dangers in
the city."

"The most dangerous thing that can happen to you here
is twisting your ankle on the cobbles," Lady Agnes assured
her. "We are a most law-abiding community. Enjoy your
walk, my dear. No need to hurry back. Dinner may be a few
minutes late since Sir Alasdair is still trying to wrest some
sense out of the rent roll."

"Sir Alasdair is the laird?" Sparrow said, tying her own
letter neatly with the pile of invitations.

"His ancestors were clan chieftains," Lady Agnes said proudly.
"The Stuarts still own most of the land hereabouts. My husband
never turned off his tenants and sold the land to English
speculators as so many did. Neither his father nor his grand-

father would ever have indulged in such a betrayal. Put a warm cloak on for the wind becomes chilly towards evening."

Going to her own room to don cloak and bonnet, Sparrow experienced a sudden revulsion of feeling against the role into which she had been forced. The Stuarts were excellent people and she felt shabby being here under false pretences. She hoped that Marie Sinclair would send an immediate reply telling her to return to London, and she trusted that she would be on her way south again before Miss Marchmont's substitute arrived.

The wind was certainly sharper when she stepped out of doors. She walked briskly down the drive and turned off onto the bridle path that led over the hill to the village. This time when she entered the semi-circle of houses one or two of the people going about their business there nodded to her briefly as if they were preparing to acknowledge her arrival in the community, and one man, riding a pony across the green, paused to greet her.

"You'll be the young lady who's come to companion Lady Agnes," he said. "Mother said she had seen you."

"Are you Tom MacGregor?" Sparrow asked.

"On my way to meet the stage as it comes south again. Would those be the invitations for the birthday?" He nodded to the packet in her hand.

"And a private letter of mine to a friend. Shall I give them to you now?"

"Lucky you caught me," he said, taking the packet. "Not all of these go south, though. I'll be needing to sort them and deliver some myself. Where does your friend live?"

"London."

"Then that'll be one for the stage. Don't fret yourself, Miss. I'll see they all get to where they're meant to go."

He nodded cheerfully, shoved the packet into his saddle-bag, and cantered off.

Feeling brighter in spirits after that amiable encounter Sparrow walked on, skirting the low hill on which the kirk and churchyard were perched and following a winding track that brought her into a maze of bracken and fern with, here, a slope of heather-clad grass and, there, a patch of sticky black peat. On the grass rough-coated sheep were grazing and in the distance she could see long-horned cattle with shaggy coats and smoke rising from an occasional farmstead. It was a pleasant rural landscape but there was a wildness under the surface, something felt but not clearly seen.

She was strolling along a narrow path bordered with gorse when a shout attracted her attention.

"Don't move one step, lassie."

A cloaked woman wearing the unlikely combination of flowered bonnet and breeches tucked into high boots was striding towards her.

"Is anything wrong?" Sparrow asked in bewilderment as the woman, rawboned and elderly, reached her side.

"You were about to step on a gin," the woman said, bending to pull aside a tussock of grass and disclosing the deadly trap. "A broken ankle is the least you could expect. Nasty, cruel things. There it goes."

With the shepherd's crook she was carrying she dealt the sprung trap a sharp blow and Sparrow flinched as the steel teeth snapped together.

"There's one hare safe for a wee while," the woman said with satisfaction. "I do what I can but the savages hereabouts cannot understand that dumb creatures feel pain too. Killing should be clean. You'll be young Lance's friend."

"And you'll be Mrs. Mackintosh." Sparrow shook hands.

"The witch Mackintosh," the other said wryly. "Well, who knows? Come and have a dish of tea with me and tell me how things are in London these days. The usurper is still mad, is he?"

"The king is—there is a Regency now," Sparrow stammered.

"With fat Georgie holding the reins. Well, the Sassenachs are welcome to him. Mind your step. The ground rises and dips without warning here. I like to dwell in a hollow with bushes about. Then my neighbours can amuse themselves wondering what I'm up to!"

She thrust aside the overhanging branches of a gnarled tree and Sparrow saw, hidden almost by the bushes that clustered thickly around it, a stone cottage with a patch of garden in which the plants spilled carelessly over the sagging fence and climbed over the cottage itself almost to the eaves.

"Warm in winter, cool in summer," Mrs. Mackintosh said. "Come along in, lassie."

The cottage was surprisingly neat and trim, woven rugs covering the stone wall, the walls hung with bunches of dried grasses, a fire burning with two rocking chairs drawn up at each side of the hearth. Between the two chairs a large tortoiseshell cat reigned supreme. In one wall a curtained alcove betokened the existence of a closet bed, and a cooking range at the back held an assortment of pots and pans. In one corner, covered with an embroidered cloth, was a square footstool on top of which a white kid glove lay.

"Make yourself easy," Mrs. Mackintosh invited. "The kettle is always boiling. If I drank as much whiskey as I do tea I'd be falling down drunk half the day. How do you come to know Lance?"

"In London," Sparrow said, taking one of the rocking chairs and wondering somewhat uneasily exactly what Lance had said.

"He said you were a very kind lady but not the charity kind," Mrs. Mackintosh said. "Made me want to meet you, and there aren't many people I'd choose to meet these days. You take sugar?"

"One spoonful, please."

Sparrow accepted the black and steaming brew and Mrs. Mackintosh sat down in the other chair.

"How do you like working for the Stuarts?" she enquired. "Fine, loyal old family, even if Sir Alasdair has a hair-trigger temper. Heart in the right place though. Of course neither of them have been the same since Adam went."

"Went?" Sparrow queried.

"Shot himself. Foolish boy to run over the moor with his

gun uncocked. Tripped, you know. Right through the head, and his poor mother just turning her face to the wall and dying, and then David rushing into wedlock with a slip of a thing and her dying when Peter came along. We all wondered where it would end."

"There was never any doubt of Adam's being dead, I suppose?" Sparrow ventured.

"Good Lord, lass," the other said. "What bee flew into that pretty bonnet you have on? I was first on the scene, just before Morag came running over the hill. He was very dead. A fine, strong lad too. Yes, it was a heavy time."

"But Peter seems a nice boy," Sparrow said, sipping her tea and hoping her tongue wouldn't end up too blistered.

"Clever too," said Mrs. Mackintosh. "He'll be away to school soon, more's the pity. You are looking at the glove."

Sparrow's eyes had indeed strayed in that direction. The white kid glove looked as if it had been deliberately placed on the footstool, not merely thrown down there and forgotten.

"It's a very expensive glove," she said awkwardly.

"Fit for the hand of a prince, eh?" The widow smiled. "And it was worn by one, lassie. By Bonnie Prince Charlie himself when he came to Edinburgh to gather the clans. My own mother was invited to the balls that were held to welcome the lad. And the prince danced with her twice. He gave her his glove as a memento and then he rode away, after telling her that one day he would be back to claim it."

"And now he never will," Sparrow said sadly, thinking of lost causes and the massacre of the clans at Culloden.

"Of course he will come back," Mrs. Mackintosh said firmly. "Of course he will return!"

"But Culloden was during the 'Forty-Five," Sparrow began and was silenced by a pitying smile.

"Time," said Mrs. Mackintosh, "does not exist when there is a wrong to be righted. You are wondering about the stool."

Sparrow was not but didn't venture to contradict.

"My mother embroidered the cushion for it," the other

returned. Well, she was not destined to see him rest his seat upon it, but that privilege is reserved for myself."

Sparrow managed a smile and drank her tea. The elderly woman was not a witch, if such beings existed, which she doubted, but a woman with a crazy streak running through her. The Prince for whom she was waiting had died of a stroke nearly twenty-five years before, before Sparrow's birth. There was no possibility of his ever returning.

"I hope Lance is behaving well," she said, seeking to change the subject.

"I like boys," Mrs. Mackintosh said. "Never had any bairns of my own, and young company livens up the place. He's away now mending a plough, though I doubt if he'll make a neat job of it, but it keeps him out of mischief."

"Well, it was kind of you to take him on." Sparrow rose, not wishing to outstay her welcome.

"Come and see me again," the other invited, also rising. "I hope you will still be here when the Prince arrives. And take care where you walk."

"Gin traps," Sparrow said.

"They are the least of it," Mrs. Mackintosh said and opened the door.

Glancing back to wave, Sparrow saw her standing there, the big cat now purring about her ankles. As Sparrow made her way out onto the moor again she beheld a familiar figure who came running towards her.

"Was you coming to see me, Miss?" Lance demanded eagerly.

"Well, not exact—" Sparrow took a second look at his hopeful face and amended her sentence. "I wondered how you were getting on. Mrs. Mackintosh seems very pleased with your efforts."

"She ain't got nobody to do for her," he deprecated. " 'Cos she's a witch, you see."

"I doubt she is any such thing," Sparrow reproved. "She is old and a little eccentric."

"She's waiting for that prince fellow to turn up," Lance

"She's waiting for that prince fellow to turn up," Lance aid. "D'ye reckon 'e will?"

"I think it highly unlikely," Sparrow said dryly. "You'd best go and see what else she needs you to do."

"Are they treating you proper up at the big 'ouse?" he paused to enquire.

"Very proper," Sparrow said, smilingly. "Now I must hurry back there." She raised her hand and hurried off, noticing that her shadow was already long on the turf. She had gained the level ground when she saw another familiar figure walking towards her.

"Lady Agnes asked me to check that you had not met with any accident," Charles Roe said.

"Does she require me for something? She said there was no hurry so I took a short walk on the moor," Sparrow said, quickening her step further.

"There was no hurry," he assured her, "but she feared that you might get lost. I know that sounds unlikely but for someone used to city life this rural district can be confusing. And there's always the danger of a haar—"

"Of a what?"

"A haar," he repeated. "Scottish for a thick mist that rolls in from nowhere with no warning. Even people who know the moors well are sometimes lost on them if a haar descends."

"Not to mention getting caught in gin traps," Sparrow said. "Life in the country sounds positively dangerous."

"The gin is a vicious instrument," Charles Roe said. "I detest cruelty to any living thing."

"Didn't you say that you were a military man?" she countered.

"Soldiers are not cruel, Miss Sparrow. They merely obey orders."

"Do you find a great difference between being a tutor and a soldier?"

"Sometimes I think it is less wearing on the feet but more wearing on the nerves," he said wryly. "Not that I mean to complain of my pupil. Peter is a splendid lad, but still a handful. I think they are right to send him to school. He misses companions of his own age."

"And then you will take another post?" She glanced at him questioningly, wondering if his handsome carriage would be regarded as an asset or not by prospective employers. As far as she knew governesses were not encouraged to be too pretty, but it might be different for their masculine counterparts.

"I have not yet given serious consideration to the matter," he replied. "What will you do when the estimable Miss Marchmont arrives with her leg healed?"

"Go back to London," Sparrow said, reminded of her somewhat precarious position in the household. Apropos of that she said, "When does the next stage from London arrive?"

"The Tuesday coach arrives on Thursday, I believe. Are you expecting someone?"

"Nobody that I know," Sparrow said truthfully.

Inwardly she breathed a small sigh of relief. Unless the genuine substitute had taken other means of transport she still had time in which to find out more—if there were any more to find out. The absolute certainty of Adam Stuart's death had brought her up against a blank wall.

"The celebrations for Sir Alasdair's birthday should be exciting," he observed. "His reputation as a fair landlord is well established, I understand. Certainly he has been a most generous employer, better than the army authorities. Mind your step."

He had noticed the trailing root of a tree too late. Even as his hand shot out Sparrow found herself on her hands and knees.

"My dear Miss Sparrow, are you hurt?" he was demanding.

She shook her head slightly to clear it and sat back on her heels, examining the palms of her hands with a wincing expression.

"A few scrapes and the seam of my gown is split," she answered ruefully. "Otherwise I am in one piece, I believe. That was stupid of me."

"I did warn you the ground could be treacherous," he said, "but I blame myself for not being sharper of eye."

"There's no harm done." She hastily retrieved her reticule, which had flown from her wrist and snapped open in its flight. "My father would tease me that I had been sampling the local whiskey. Thank you, Mr. Roe."

He had helped her to her feet and bent to pick up something that had fluttered from her reticule. Sparrow held out her hand but he went on holding the object, his fair head bent.

"Mr. Roe?" She spoke his name warily, conscious of a sudden tension in the set of his shoulders.

"You dropped your handkerchief, I think." He returned it to her, his dark eyes flashing to her face with a look that pierced her through and through.

"Thank you." She scrubbed unavailingly at her grazed palms and then gave up the attempt. She would have to apply remedies when she had reached her room. She thrust the handkerchief up her sleeve and pulled her cloak more tightly round her, hearing another ominous tearing sound as the seam of her dress split further.

"If you will excuse me," Charles Roe said abruptly, "I must return to my pupil. I left him colouring in a map of the world and he will have added further countries beyond those in existence to while away the time. You know the way from here."

His bow was brief and careless and then he was striding ahead of her up the drive, moving so rapidly that she could not have been blamed for thinking that he wished to escape from her.

Sparrow followed him slowly, her brow creased in a worried frown. Something had definitely discomposed the tutor. She stood still, tugging over the handkerchief again, looking at the embroidered black bow with the ends turned back upon themselves. Marie Sinclair's handkerchief was merely a handkerchief. Apart from the unusual monogram in one corner it was exactly like any other kerchief. Neither was the monogram as unfamiliar as it had seemed when she had first opened the message left for her in the stagecoach office. In the office she had dropped the coins and Simon Adair had been there to help her pick them up. He too had stared down at the handkerchief before returning it to her and, after that, his manner too had changed. She frowned more intently, trying in vain to recall where she had seen that particular design before, but the answer eluded her.

Well, there was no sense in standing stock-still. She thrust the handkerchief up her sleeve again and went on, somewhat shakily, as the shock of the fall registered itself on her nerves.

"Miss Sparrow, are you all right?"

Peter emerged suddenly from the bend in the path ahead of her.

"Yes, I—you saw me stumble?"

"No, I only just got here," he informed her. "I wondered why you were standing still with such a peculiar look on your face."

"I was thinking," she said absently. "Did you finish colouring your picture of the world?"

"Ages ago," he informed her. "I invented some new countries and put them in the middle of the oceans, and then I came out to see if Mr. Roe was on his way back. I hope you were not hurt when you stumbled?"

"Only my dignity," Sparrow said. "You like your tutor very much, don't you? It will be hard when the time comes for you to go to school after being with him for so long."

"Three months isn't so long," Peter said.

"Three months?" Sparrow, who had begun to walk forward again, paused and looked at him.

"He came at the end of March," Peter said. "Perhaps the beginning of April. I forget."

"Who was your tutor before?" Sparrow asked, beginning to walk on again.

"I did lessons with the minister and some of them with Aunt Agnes," the child informed her.

"But it was decided you needed extra tuition before you went to school?"

"No, I don't think so." Peter looked slightly bewildered. "I came down one morning and Mr. Roe was there. Uncle Alasdair said he was my tutor, and Mr. Roe smiled and said he looked forward to working with me. Except that he doesn't much—I mean he spends lots of time talking with Uncle Alasdair so I do pretty much as I please."

Sparrow was silent as they went towards the house. Marie Sinclair's sweetheart had come up to Scotland three months before. Charles Roe had been definitely shaken when he had picked up the handkerchief, probably recognising it as one of Marie's. If Marie's letters had arrived at Craig Bothwell it would have been a fairly simple matter for the tutor to purloin and destroy them. Perhaps Charles Roe had pretended to a relationship with the people who were going to be his employers when in fact he was only the tutor, but he would have had to possess knowledge that there had been a real Adam Stuart and it didn't strike her as the kind of information one gave out when selecting a tutor for a small boy.

At the front door Peter ran off, presumably to find his tutor, and she went on alone up the stairs, meeting Morag on her way out of the gallery.

"Mr. Roe said you took a wee tumble," she said. "I put hot water and some of my mother's salve in a jar there. It's very good for cuts and scrapes."

"Thank you, Morag. My dress was worse hurt than I was."

"If you lay it across the chair I'll see to the mending of it while you're at dinner," Morag said obligingly.

Sparrow thanked her again and went on into her room. The lamps had been kindled and their reflections danced in the clear panes of window glass. She went over to the window and leaned her forehead against the cold glass. Below her the herb garden was silvery in the twilight, the paths shell edged, winding round like bows with the ends tucked back. Staring down at the revealed pattern she felt a new bewilderment seize her. The pattern made by the curving beds was the same as the pattern in the corner of Marie Sinclair's handkerchief.

= 8 =

SHE HAD MADE up her mind that she was probably safe until
the stagecoach arrived on the following Thursday when, it
was almost certain, the real substitute for Miss Marchmont
would render it necessary for her to offer an explanation,
unless she could find some proof that Charles Roe was the
man who had called himself Adam Stuart to Marie Sinclair.
The problem was that, as far as she knew, there was no law
against a handsome young man lying to a lady he wished
to impress, and so far she had seen nothing that might
suggest he was engaged in anything illegal.

Yet the sense of there being something more for her to
discover hung over her like a shadow. For the next few days she
felt as if she were walking on ground that might suddenly turn
into black bog beneath her feet. Some of it was probably due
to her own imagination but she was sure she was not imagining
the changed attitude of the tutor towards her. He had been
charming before and he was still charming, but his dark eyes
rested on her too often and too speculatively. Whatever he was
thinking he was evidently keeping to himself since she saw no
alteration in the attitudes of Sir Alasdair and Lady Agnes.

The former was out and about much of the time, riding
to inspect the tenant farms that were part of the estate, and
he spent two or three hours a day closeted with Charles
Roe, whom he continued to treat more like an honoured
guest than an employee. Lady Agnes was immersed in plans
for the celebrations, and the house was being cleaned and
polished to within an inch of its life by various women,

armed with mops and buckets, being directed by Morag, while from the kitchen wafted the scents of baking. Peter was here, there, and everywhere, more in evidence than he had been when she first arrived.

"There hasn't been a party at Craig Bothwell for years," Lady Agnes told her, as they sat in one of the downstairs sitting-rooms carefully decorating menu cards. "Peter is very excited about it all."

"He doesn't have birthday parties?" Sparrow looked up in surprise.

"We never had the heart," Lady Agnes said sadly. "So many unfortunate things happened round about the time when Peter was born that we have never been able to regard it with unmitigated joy."

"His half brother dying three years before?" Sparrow ventured.

"Adam, yes." Lady Agnes drew a deep breath and shook her powdered head. "Such a lovely lad. It killed his mother. And then David married again, and when Peter was born she died and David went back to sea and got himself killed. A very sad time indeed. Peter is the sole heir of our house, yet we cannot bring ourselves to celebrate his birth. Now, shall we add silver bells in the margins or would that be too ostentatious?"

"I am wondering where everybody is to be seated," Sparrow said.

"Oh, the dinner will be for close associates," Lady Agnes said. "No more than forty-five or so, and the villagers will have refreshments sent down to them. The ball is for all to attend. We shall pray for a good evening so that the bonfire and fireworks will not be ruined by rain. So far this summer we have been most fortunate."

Which still left more than fifty of the hundred or so invited guests to be fed somewhere or other, Sparrow thought, dipping her pen into the silver ink.

"It is to be hoped that you will attend the ball," Lady Agnes said a moment later.

The ball but not the dinner. Sparrow felt an unreasonable spasm of disappointment just as a voice said from the doorway, "Surely you will invite this lovely young lady to sit down with us, Lady Agnes? I swear I will not enjoy a mouthful if she is banished to her room."

"Oh, of course, if you wish it, Mr. Roe. I did of course expect Miss Sparrow to attend the dinner. It was understood."

"Splendid." His smile included them both. "Peter has asked for you, Lady Agnes. He is complaining of a loose tooth, which he refuses to believe is entirely natural for his age."

"Cotton and a doorknob," Lady Agnes said in a distracted manner, rising. "Sparrow, can you complete the rest of the menus—unless Mr. Roe desires your company?" She looked from one to the other and rustled out.

Sparrow bent her head again and carefully outlined another bell.

"Your company would indeed be most pleasant," Charles Roe said softly.

"I have work to do," Sparrow said firmly. The family might treat him as a guest but she was determined to regard him in the same light as herself, as an employee.

"Do it later," he said. "At this moment I would enjoy your company."

"Mr. Roe, Lady Agnes employs me," she replied sharply. "I prefer to finish these first, and I imagine that you will be anxious to get back to your pupil."

"Small boys with loose teeth were never a particularly favourite occupation of mine," he said.

"Then you ought not to have become a tutor," she said, and blushed angrily as he put back his head and laughed.

"How prim and English you sound," he exclaimed. "You know, I have been wondering how a lovely young girl like yourself becomes a companion, but now I see that you are a man-hater."

"Indeed I am not!" She dug her pen into the menu card, uttered an unladylike expletive occasionally let slip by her father, and bit her lip.

"Why not come for a short stroll?" he invited more coaxingly. "You have been busy every day since Sunday and there is surely no harm in taking advantage of her ladyship's kindness for an hour?"

"Very well." Rising, she reminded herself that on the next evening the stagecoach would be there, and might well be disgorging a lone female passenger.

"You disapprove of me?" He cast her a brightly mocking look as they went out together.

"Not at all," she said untruthfully. "I never even think of you, Mr. Roe."

"I have been thinking of you a great deal," he said. "You strike me as a most unusual young woman, full of an independent spirit that takes little account of convention."

"You are wrong. I am very conventional."

'Yet you leave your home in the south and come up over the border to take a temporary post in what is, surely by your standards, a most backward and primitive region."

"And you give up a wandering life as a soldier in order to tutor a small boy in the same place."

"I thought you never allowed me to enter you mind," he said.

Sparrow found herself laughing despite her resolve.

"That's better." He moved a few inches closer. "Grim disapproval does not become you."

"I do not approve of flirtation," she said primly, and thought with a sudden, sharp longing of Simon Adair, which was ridiculous since she had never flirted with him and didn't expect to meet him again.

"Do you not? I find it a delightful pastime," he said mildly.

She wished she had the courage to say, "Did you regard your relationship with Marie Sinclair as a delightful pastime?" but to do that would be to reveal herself too plainly.

"It is much warmer in Scotland than I expected," she said instead.

"Ah, we are to confine our conversation to the weather, are we?" He gave her another glinting smile. "For the time of year it is indeed very warm and dry. Now what shall we talk about?"

"The sermon preached in the kirk on Sunday morning was very interesting."

"The Reverend Laurie has a way with words, hasn't he? He is not from this area and so, even after twenty years, is regarded still as a newcomer," Charles Roe said. "If he took a wife the villagers would like him better. Do you fancy being a clergyman's wife?"

"Not at all," Sparrow said with decision. "I could never live up to the image."

"Yet one day some fortunate man will snap you up."

"Like a bargain in the marketplace? Thank you, but I prefer my independence. I notice that you do too."

"But I love the fair sex,"he said sadly. "It is a great pity that so many of the lovely ladies are so obsessed with the ambition to get a wedding ring on their fingers."

She walked on without comment, wondering if he were sounding a warning. If so, it was quite unnecessary in her case.

"In London," he went on musingly, "the ladies have a certain elegance that one does not find anywhere else save possibly in Paris."

"You have visited London recently?" Sparrow asked the question as casually as she could.

"About three months ago." He answered with equal casualness. "It was my first visit for many years. I travelled there as a boy after my studies were finished."

"From Germany?"

"From Germany, where I was educated."

"You were born in England though?"

"In France. The Revolution broke out when I was nine, and I was taken to Germany by friends."

Which made him twenty-seven, Sparrow quickly calculated, the same age Adam Stuart would be, had he lived.

"Charles Roe is not a French name, is it?" she enquired.

"It can be. The wind is rising, Miss Sparrow. You have no cloak or bonnet. Shall we turn back?"

They had almost reached the end of the drive. Sparrow turned obediently, forcing a smile as her eye met the tutor's searching gaze.

"You were born in London?" was all he said.

"Yes." She hesitated, then deeming it only fair that she should volunteer a little information after asking so many questions herself added, "My mother died and I have lived with my father ever since save for time I spent at a school for girls."

"And this is your first visit to Scotland?"

She nodded, casting him a questioning look.

"Scotland is certainly a beautiful country," he said, but there was a dying fall to his tone that made the comment melancholy.

"And still living in the past," she said. "I met an elderly lady who has a glove that Bonnie Prince Charlie gave to her mother, promising to return and claim it one day, and though she seems quite sane in every other respect she still keeps the glove in expectation of his coming."

"The Widow Mackintosh. I have met the lady. She has a local, probably undeserved, reputation as a witch. Do you speak French, Miss Sparrow?"

"Yes, quite fluently," Sparrow said, bewildered by the sudden change of subject. "We had an excellent teacher at school and my father often insisted on my speaking it with him."

"It is a melodious language. We must speak it together sometime. Now I must attend my pupil."

They had arrived at the house again and he bowed somewhat hastily and hurried within. Sparrow stared after him for a moment or two. She was almost completely convinced that he was Marie Sinclair's missing sweetheart, but that knowledge was getting her nowhere. What was so peculiar was that he seemed almost equally interested in her own history, drawing her out to talk of her school and her father. And he had given no adequate explanation as to how he had come to be employed as tutor in the Stuart family.

Despite the cold wind she felt no inclination to return within doors and turned instead in the direction of the herb garden, skirting the wall and approaching the ivy-clad keep. Until this moment she had not walked in this part of the grounds, and her footsteps slowed as she went over the rough grass towards the stone tower. Certainly it looked solid enough, though she had been warned that it was crumbling. There were the outlines of the foundation of some lower building at the side of the structure, probably a barn to judge from the pale rectangle with its shards of broken stone and tile that marked the site clearly amid the brighter green of the surrounding foliage.

There was one door in the keep, an arched oaken door with a heavy iron knocker. Above, the thin slits of window reminded her of earlier, less civilised days. This had been the home of the Stuart family until about a hundred years before. No doubt the thick creeper hid any ancient marks of fire or sword incurred during those almost forgotten border raids. She pushed the heavy door idly and almost jumped out of her skin when it immediately swung slowly inward.

A round room with a stone staircase spiralling up out of its centre met her gaze. In the past, animals and stores would have been kept here, she supposed, while the living quarters were above ground, the family eating together and sleeping in curtained-off sections that afforded a minimum of privacy. At school the history mistress had been more interested in the domestic details of past living than in the dates of battles and reigns.

The stone staircase had a stout iron handrail and the steps, though worn, were uncracked. Sparrow hesitated, then stepped forward, testing the handrail and finding it firmly stapled into the stone. There didn't seem anything unsafe about the staircase at all, but possibly the upper storey with its floor of wooden planks was dangerous.

The spiralling stairs ended abruptly at a shallow landing with a low archway cut out of the stone wall. Sparrow placed her foot hesitantly on the timber and found it sturdy.

The archway was so low that, though she was smaller than average, she had to bend her head. Within the archway was a narrow antechamber darkened by heavy velvet curtains drawn across the farther side. Biting her lip, she stared at the drapes. Whatever else was old in this place these were certainly not. They were clearly new and clean, hung from a brass curtain rod that had only recently been affixed.

She lifted one edge of the curtain and stepped cautiously within. The timbers under her feet were rock firm and beeswaxed, the scent of it lingering. The upper storey was also roughly circular in shape with window embrasures wide and deep enough to fit beds, but they contained only stools. Between two of the narrow apertures sat a carved chair cushioned in white silk with black motifs embroidered on it, a white silk canopy fringed in gold above it. Without much surprise she recognised the distinctive bow again. The light slanting through the windows was not strong enough to illumine every corner. A table in one embrasure held a row of lamps, each one trimmed and oil filled. Sparrow debated whether or not to risk lighting one from the tinder box beside them but her eyes were growing accustomed to the gloom and she decided against it.

Footsteps were coming up the stairs beyond the curtain. Quick, light footsteps. She looked desperately around for somewhere to conceal herself but there was nowhere. Then the curtain was lifted and a figure smaller and slighter than herself came in.

"I saw you coming in," Peter said, "so I followed you. Morag forgot to lock the door, I think."

"Morag Og?" Sparrow said stupidly.

"She and Angus have been preparing the place," Peter said. "I'm not supposed to know, but I sometimes hear what little pigs are not supposed to hear—as Aunt Agnes often remarks."

"Preparing it for what?" Sparrow asked in bewilderment.

"For the Prince," Peter said, lowering his voice and giving a capital letter to the word. "He is coming back to claim his throne."

"Are you talking about Bonnie Prince Charlie?" Sparrow demanded. "If you are then I can tell you that—"

"It is a great secret," Peter interrupted. "You mustn't tell anyone. About his coming or this place, I mean. Especially not Mr. Roe."

"Why not Mr. Roe?" she enquired.

Peter lifted his narrow shoulders in a creditable imitation of an adult shrug.

"I heard Aunt Agnes say to Morag, 'We must keep Mr. Roe away from the keep at all costs,' and Morag smiled and said 'Yes, My Lady.' I have never been up here myself. I thought it wasn't safe."

"It seems safe enough," Sparrow said. "But, Peter, what you are suggesting simply isn't—"

"My tooth came out." He opened his mouth to show her. "Aunt Agnes tied cotton around it and tied the other end to the kitchen door handle and it came out clean as a whistle."

"That's splendid, but —"

"And after the ordeal I was not in the mood for lessons, so I slipped out by the side door and saw you coming this way and so I followed you. Shall we go back in case anyone is looking for us?"

It struck Sparrow as an excellent idea. The prospect of being discovered prying was not an appealing one.

"I suppose the Prince will be coming here," Peter said as they went out again down the stairs.

"He will have to have a throne room until he rides into Edinburgh and is crowned."

If anyone had ever told him that Prince Charles Edward Stuart was dead he had chosen to forget it.

"Morag will be back soon to lock the door," the child continued as they left the keep. There was a large iron key on the inside of the door.

"Perhaps someone saw us coming here?" Sparrow looked somewhat apprehensively towards the house beyond the wall.

"Not they!" Peter gave a scornful little sniff.

"Why not?"

"Uncle Alasdair is away with Angus to check the salmon, and Mr. Roe will be flirting with Aunt Agnes."

"Peter!"

"Mr. Roe flirts with all the ladies," Peter said, undeterred by her shocked disapproval. "Mr. Roe is very fond of the ladies."

Sparrow decided it was prudent to abandon the subject. Her head was already whirling with the pieces of information entering it.

Bonnie Prince Charlie was dead, except that he was expected here shortly. Mr. Roe was almost certainly Adam Stuart or calling himself so three months before. But he was not part of whatever was going on at Craig Bothwell since he was being kept away from the keep. Nothing made any sense at all.

She was relieved when Peter ran off to reveal himself to his tutor and she could return to the sitting-room, where nothing more mentally demanding awaited her than the completion of the menus.

The next evening the coach was due from London, no doubt containing the real replacement for the unfortunate Miss Marchmont. Considering the situation, Sparrow told herself that, in actual fact, she had fulfilled her promise to Marie Sinclair.

Mr. Roe must be the same young man who had made love to Marie Sinclair under the pseudonym of Adam Stuart. Possibly in the course of correspondence between him and Sir Alasdair, before he took up his appointment as Peter's tutor, something had been mentioned about the real Adam Stuart and Charles Roe had merely borrowed the name. It had been a mite careless of him to give his current lady love the correct address of the place to which he was travelling, but he might not have expected her to take his attentions so seriously.

As for whatever else was happening that was none of her business whatsoever, Sparrow continued to ponder it. Loyalty to the Stuarts was clearly very strong in the district as it was still strong in many parts of Scotland, but she had always assumed that it was a sentimental souvenir of days gone by since the Stuarts were dead. Yet the firm expectations of the Widow Mackintosh and the room now prepared in the old keep hinted at something more than sentiment.

For the remainder of that evening and most of the next day she was busy dealing with plans for flower arrangements—"Heather and bluebells with some of those tiny wild lilies one finds growing near the bogs, dear," Lady Agnes instructed.

Offering to go out and pick them herself, Sparrow cast a wary eye at the clock, imagining the stagecoach lumbering its way over the border. If she met the stage perhaps she could talk to Miss Marchmont's replacement and persuade her to return, offer her half of the money she still had in her reticule. The idea pleased her more than sitting waiting for discovery and, having pleaded a headache that was not entirely an untruth, she went upstairs to don cloak and bonnet.

It was a temptation to veer in the direction of the keep and take another look there, but common sense told her that by now it would be locked again. Instead she walked with an elaborately casual air down the drive between the high banks of gorse.

The stagecoach was early. She could see the lead horses straining up the last part of the hill before they gained the level ground that ran past the gates of Craig Bothwell. The light was only just beginning to fade, and coach and horses were outlined against the sky like a silhouette cut from black paper. She held her breath as the horses approached, and let it out again in a long, disbelieving sigh of relief as they swerved and trotted past. No passenger had asked to be set down at Craig Bothwell, which meant that for some reason the replacement hadn't arrived. She still had time to find out, for her own satisfaction if for nothing else, what on earth was going on.

She watched the stage until it was out of sight and then began to walk in the direction of the village. At least it was safe for a solitary lady to walk in these parts without interference, she mused. In London the level of violence had risen alarmingly.

Almost as that comfortable thought crossed her mind there was a sharp crack and a shower of little stones was flung up slightly to the right of her. For an instant she stared at the tumbling pebbles, then swung round. The road was empty but she had the walls of the estate on her right and the shot—she was convinced it had been a shot—had come from behind them. She ran to the wall, hitched up her skirt, and began to clamber up, thanking Providence for the jutting stones that made it easy to obtain a foothold.

Gripping the top she raised her head cautiously and peered over, but the thick shrubbery showed no telltale sign of movement. Whoever was there might, of course, still be hiding, repriming his pistol.

That uncomfortable thought was sufficient to send her scrabbling for a foothold so that she could descend. Unhappily, her narrow skirt had been made for gentle walking, not for climbing up walls, and there was an ominous ripping sound that made her look down in dismay. The man who had walked quietly along the grass verge and now stood below her on the road grinned up at her engagingly.

"Are you waiting for a mudlark to come along?" Simon Adair enquired.

=== 9 ===

"Don't you dare to laugh at my predicament!" She slithered down the rest of the wall in a rush and landed, willy-nilly, in Simon's arms. Glowering up at the harsh face lit now by teasing mirth, she couldn't decide if she was more glad or sorry to see him.

"You do make a habit of balancing on high places, don't you?" he said in a conversational tone, giving her a little hug before he released her. "Are you training to be a mountaineer?"

"Someone took a shot at me," she exclaimed.

"Oh? Are you such a terrible governess as all that?"

"Oh, don't joke. Someone really did shoot at me from behind the wall and that's why I was climbing up to see, but there isn't anyone there now."

"Grouse shooting?" He cocked a dark eyebrow.

"On the main road in the wrong month? No, someone really did shoot at me."

"Then the bullet will be around somewhere. Where were you?"

"A few yards further on. And where were you?" she demanded suddenly.

"Not behind the wall shooting at you," he said, beginning to walk up the road, his head bent. "Actually I was on the stage and I got off at the corner and walked back. Ah, here it is." With an exclamation of satisfaction he picked up a small, flattened piece of metal and looked at it and then glanced towards the wall again.

"Where were you when you heard the shot?" he asked abruptly.

"About here. The stones flew up."

"Whoever fired at you must have had a remarkably bad aim to miss at that distance," Simon said. "Or he had a remarkably good aim and was just trying to frighten you."

"He succeeded," she said shortly. "Simon, what are you doing here?"

"May I assume that your charming use of my Christian name means we are now on terms of intimate friendship?"

"You may not assume anything at all. And you haven't answered my question."

"You first," he invited.

"I beg your pardon?"

"What are you doing here? Not teaching the little lads who suddenly required a governess, I'll be bound. And not staying with your dear old school friend."

"You've met my father."

"I called to enquire after his health and was invited to take a drink with him. His daughter was in Scotland, visiting friends, he told me. Your housekeeper, Mrs. O'Hara, looked as if she were choking on a fishbone and seized the first opportunity to inform me privately that you were employed as a temporary governess."

"As I told you," she reminded him.

"Except that Craig Bothwell has only one child within its walls and you are not his governess."

"How do you know that?" she challenged.

"I got talking to someone somewhere or other," he said vaguely. "So what are you doing here?"

"I am companion to Lady Agnes—not that it is any concern of yours, Mr. Adair."

"What happened to Simon?" he wanted to know.

"Simon was when I was somewhat discomposed," she said with dignity. "Now I am quite at ease."

"Is that why you are biting your lower lip and wondering whether or not to tell me the full story?" he asked.

He had hit so near the truth that she blushed, saying hastily, "I came out to gather lilies and it will be dark soon. We must step onto the moor in order to find them."

"Then by all means," he said promptly, "let us gather lilies together. Delightful occupation. Where does one find them?"

"Near the patches of bog."

"I was afraid you might say something like that." He glanced at his boots and tight nankeen trousers and then grinned again. "Lead on then, and you can tell me how two small boys turned into Lady Agnes."

It was a big temptation to confide in him, but she resisted it, reminding herself that his arrival on the scene had been a trifle too opportune and that he had, as yet, given no explanation for his coming. The suspicion that he had chased after her for some romantic reason was swiftly banished when she recalled the lady with the feathered hat.

"Oh, Tizzie would never have countenanced my being at the beck and call of an elderly woman," she said, "so I invented the little boys. However, it is a perfectly respectable temporary position and I will be returning to London very soon. Now will you kindly tell me—?"

"Are those the flowers you are seeking?" he broke in, pointing to a patch of cloudy white.

"Yes, but—"

"Stay where you are. The ground looks very marshy hereabouts and your dress is already torn. He strode off, stepping rapidly from one tussock of firm turf to the next, stooping to pick the blossoms while she clenched her fists in exasperation. He obviously had no intention of giving her a straight story, which meant that, in some way, he was part of whatever was going on here.

"There we are." He was returning, a bunch of the delicate flowers trembling in his hand. "They are certainly very lovely. You ought to wear one or two in your hair."

"At the ball," she said unwarily.

"There is to be a ball?"

"A celebration for Sir Alasdair's seventy-fifth birthday," she said reluctantly. "There are various neighbours and friends coming, so I cannot imagine where you are hoping to find lodging."

"Oh, there is a tavern here and there, I believe," he said, beginning to walk back with her towards the road. "You must not fret yourself about my welfare."

"I am quite sure that you can look after yourself," she said dryly, accepting the flowers, trying not to notice how his fingers brushed hers in the passing.

"I wish I were as confident about your own capabilities," he retorted. "Try not to go walking alone near walls over the next few days. *Au revoir*, Sparrow."

And before she could question further he was gone, striding up the long road without a backward look.

His coming was neither romantic nor a coincidence, she mused, repressing a feeling of disappointment that had risen in her without warning. He had doubtless tricked Tizzie or her father into revealing her address, but she was almost convinced that he had known the place in some connection that had nothing to do with her presence here. And he had known more, or guessed more, about the shooting than he was willing to reveal.

She went slowly back to the house, feeling a tremor of unaccustomed nervousness as she passed the walls of the herb garden with the ivied keep rising beyond, but nothing untoward happened.

Morag, meeting her in the hall, said pleasantly, "Och, but I always did love those flowers. Mind, the heather and the bluebells are grand too. Lady Agnes will be wanting them kept in moss until it's time to decorate the tables."

She took the blooms and turned back to the kitchen quarters, pausing as Sparrow said, "Is everybody out?"

"Lady Agnes is hearing Master Peter recite his poem," Morag said, "and my father just now came back from the river with Sir Alasdair, and Mr. Roe is—marking exercises in the schoolroom, I think. Were you wanting any of them?"

"No, it's only that—"

"You've torn your dress again," Morag exclaimed suddenly.

"I seem to be making a habit of it, don't I?" Sparrow said ruefully. "Morag, someone shot at me when I was walking along the road outside the gates."

Whoever the mysterious marksman had been it certainly hadn't been Morag, who looked completely horrified, the colour fading so sharply from her face that her freckles stood out clearly.

"Oh, Miss, that's dreadful," she exclaimed. "Are you certain sure?"

"Absolutely," Sparrow said firmly.

"But I cannot—oh, you cannot be thinking that someone from the house took a shot at you?"

"The shot came from over the wall of the estate," Sparrow said.

"Then it's poachers," Morag said, a note of relief in her voice. "If they're not after the salmon they're after the coneys or the pheasants."

Sparrow was inclined to argue that even the most short-sighted poacher could scarcely have mistaken her for a coney or a pheasant, but she judged it wiser to hold her tongue on the matter, saying only, "Perhaps I was mistaken. Don't mention it to anyone else. I would hate to cause a fuss over nothing, particularly as—"

"Adam was shot," Morag finished for her. "Since then everybody has been so careful about firearms. Why, Sir Alasdair keeps his rifles and pistols under lock and key until the grouse shooting begins and then he is very cautious about giving them out. No, you were mistaken, Miss. Now, if you'll change your dress I'll see to the mending of it."

"Really, you don't have to bother," Sparrow began but was interrupted heartily.

"Sewing is never a bother, Miss Sparrow, especially when you have such fine garments. I was only saying to my mother that it's plain you are new to earning your living with clothes that many a grand lady would be happy to wear."

"Oh, it is only that I am generally careful with them and so they last a long time," Sparrow told her, blushing furiously.

"I'll be putting the lilies on damp moss," Morag said, "and then I'll get out my needle." She nodded brightly and went on into the kitchen.

Having changed her dress, Sparrow hesitated and then walked through the gallery and turned into the other wing where Sir Alasdair had his rooms and where Peter did lessons with his tutor. Someone had shot at her, and the person she was most inclined to suspect was Charles Roe. At least it would do not harm to ask him obliquely and note his first unguarded reaction. The door of the schoolroom was partly open and he sat at a table, writing industriously in a notebook that he closed as she coughed gently.

"Miss Sparrow, please to come in. You have not yet visited the schoolroom." His tone was amiable. Perhaps she was imagining a certain wariness in his glance.

"I was looking for Peter," she said mendaciously. "I feel that I ought to purchase some small token for Sir Alasdair's birthday and children have splendid ideas."

"He is with Lady Agnes. Do please come in, or are memories of your own school days so full of pain that you cannot bear to do so?"

"On the contrary, I enjoyed school very much," she informed him, entering and looking round the apartment, which, despite its smart peppermint-striped cushions and thick carpet, had acquired the faintly shabby aspect of a room where a small boy spends much of his time.

"I believe Peter will enjoy going to school too," he said, "for he has an outgoing personality and will respond well to the company of other children."

"Are you from a large family yourself?" Sparrow enquired.

"I have two older sisters," he said. "It is some years since I have seen them. You?"

"Only me," Sparrow said.

"Relatives can be a great nuisance," Charles Roe said. "I often feel myself bedevilled by mine. You are attending the ball that is to be held after the dinner, are you not?"

"Lady Agnes did mention ――" Sparrow hesitated, then said boldly, "I was not going to be asked to the dinner until you suggested it."

"An oversight, I'm sure," he said.

"Lady Agnes is very anxious to please you," Sparrow said. Her eyes held a question but to her surprise Charles Roe said carelessly, "Is she? I had not particularly noticed."

"Then you certainly have not been a tutor before," Sparrow said crisply. "I understand they are usually greatly put upon and sometimes despised."

"Then I must count myself fortunate, not least that there is a delightful young lady also employed here with whom I can enjoy a charming friendship."

He was flirting with her and, for some reason she had not yet begun to analyse, she was not enjoying it at all. However, the words afforded her the opportunity to say sweetly, "I could have done with your friendship not long since. Someone took a shot at me when I went out to pick the lilies for Lady Agnes."

The wariness was as apparent as if he were waving a banner with the words "Take Care" emblazoned upon it. He looked at her silently for a moment, then said in a low, hurried tone from which all semblance of flirting had fled, "I am certain the person meant you no harm, Miss Sparrow. No harm in the world."

"You know who it was?" she demanded.

"Some careless fellow, I expect. I was here so I cannot say."

"I am hoping that whoever it was will be less careless in the future," Sparrow said darkly. "When my period of employment ends I hope to be in one piece."

"Yes, of course—surely you will be. You wished to buy something for Sir Alasdair? I am sure that such a gesture, though appreciated, would not be expected," he said. "Peter is with Lady Agnes, I believe. He is to recite a poem he has been learning for the occasion, and Lady Agnes wished to coach him in it."

"And you are preparing exercises. I will go and find Peter." Smiling slightly, she turned to leave when, to her astonishment, he seized her hand, saying in the same low, intensely nervous manner, "Please disregard what occurred earlier. When a person misses at such close range then they never meant to hit you in the first place."

"I hope not." Disengaging her hand, she thought that he was probably right, since Simon had reached the same conclusion, but Simon had had the chance to examine the location of the incident, and nothing she had said to Charles Roe could have led him to guess that the shot had been at close range. Unless he had been the marksman he had no way of knowing.

It was a disquieting thought to take back to her room, where, having made the usual vain attempt to smooth down her ruffled auburn curls, she decided to recover from her "headache" and go down to dinner.

Had she been expecting revelations she would have been disappointed. Sir Alasdair was full of complaints about the amount of refuse being flung into the river by his tenants. Lady Agnes was trying to decide if the lilies should be grouped in a centrepiece or tiny bowls of them set down the centre of the table. Neither Charles Roe nor Peter put in an appearance, though in the latter's case that was normal. Eating her roast duck, Sparrow wondered if the little boy would be permitted to attend his great-uncle's birthday dinner.

"And the walk on the moors did your megrim good?" Lady Agnes broke off her floral arranging to enquire.

"My—? Oh yes, thank you." Sparrow blushed slightly, never having been able to invent an excuse without suffering pangs of conscience. That she had spun two false yarns to both her father and Tizzie would give her sleepless nights if she allowed herself to think about it.

"Thought I caught a glimpse of you as Angus and I were coming away from the river," Sir Alasdair rumbled. "Then realised it couldn't be. Some lass with a young lad. Did you see them?"

"I don't think so," Sparrow said, blushing more furiously.

"You ought to make enquiries," Lady Agnes said, frowning slightly. "Now is not the time to have strangers wandering about."

She broke off with a quick glance towards Sparrow, who said equally hastily, "Birthdays should be for family and friends, I think."

"And our family is shrinking," Lady Agnes said sadly. "All our hopes now are centered in Peter."

"He's a good lad," Sir Alasdair pronounced. "He wouldn't go throwing rubbish into the river!"

The conversation had reverted to the sore subject of the tenants' slovenly habits, though from the perfect indifference with which Lady Agnes received her husband's strictures it was clear this was an old hobby horse which the laird rode frequently. Only once more, as one of Mrs. Og's suety puddings was placed on the table, was anything unusual said, and then it was Lady Agnes who asked Morag, "Has some pudding been sent up to Mr. Roe? One must consider his comfort."

"A special small one, my lady," Morag assured her.

"Not too small, I trust?" Lady Agnes frowned. "Mr. Roe strikes me as somewhat delicate in constitution. Too many years spent eating that dreadful foreign food, I expect."

The care they displayed for the tutor was quite extraordinary, Sparrow mused, but then she reminded herself that she too had been welcomed as if she were a relative and not merely a temporary employee. Perhaps the Stuarts simply behaved like benevolent despots because they were both slightly eccentric.

She excused herself before the coffee was served and went upstairs, hoping for a period of quietness in which to collect her scattered thoughts. Annoyingly, her mind fixed itself on the whereabouts of an exasperating man with mocking turquoise blue eyes. By now Simon Adair would doubtless have found a lodging place and would be preparing—whatever it was he was preparing.

She was certain that he had followed her and equally certain that it was not for romantic purposes, the latter certainty making her feel unaccountably irritable. No doubt he preferred ladies in feathered hats. With a little encouragement Charles Roe might fall in love with her, but apart from the fact that it would be reprehensible of her to come seeking out another lady's sweetheart only to steal him, the plain fact was that she didn't want Charles Roe for all his fair locks and dark, soulful eyes. And she reminded herself firmly that even if he hadn't been the unknown marksman, he had heard about or seen the incident.

It was impossible to sleep or even to lie down for very long. Though it was not yet ten the great house was silent. People in these parts kept early hours. She donned dressing gown and low slippers and opened her door.

Next to the Nookery was a room lined with well-filled bookshelves, not well enough equipped to be distinguished as a library but on the shelves she hoped to find something to take her mind off her present problems. If all else failed, she thought wryly, she could always hit herself over the head with a heavy tome.

The lamps had been trimmed and burnt low and steadily as she went through the gallery and down the stairs. There was no lamp in the book-lined chamber but the moon shone in through the gap between the between the drawn curtains and she had noticed on her earlier tour that several of Mrs. Radcliffe's romances were on the shelf near the window. Perhaps ruined castles and languishing heroines were not the best choice for bedtime reading, but the heroines in the novels always ended triumphant, so she might garner a few useful hints.

Taking a book, she turned to look out into the garden where the shell-edged paths bound the herb beds with sealed knots. In the moonlight, shadows had a flat, black emphasis, and the colour was drained from the green plants.

The scene was both peaceful and mysterious. It was a place, she mused, that called out for lovers to walk there. Beyond the wall light gleamed briefly from the slit windows of the keep and was as swiftly gone. Sparrow jumped nervously, then chided herself. The keep was ancient but there were no incarcerated heirs or mouldering skeletons there such as one regularly found in the pages of Mrs. Radcliffe. The place had been prepared in the latest, most modern fashion even if the person expected had been dead for more than twenty years.

A side door unbolted into the garden. She stepped out into the maze of black shadow and pale moonlight, stood for a moment uncertainly, and then walked, noiseless in her slippers, to the wicket gate that brought her into the main grounds. Here she could skirt the inner walls of the herb garden without much fear of discovery, and reach the rough grass that led to the keeps.

She stopped dead, pressing herself into the deeper shadows cast by the wall, as the main door of the keep swung slowly inwards. A lantern flashed golden fire and was quickly covered, and a figure stepped out onto the grass, followed by the more familiar outline of Morag. The latter had turned and was stooping to lock the door again. The strange figure stood, holding the lantern, then passed it to the maidservant.

"All is ready as you saw for yourself," came Morag's lilting tone through the late evening silence.

"And most fitting," her companion said. "We are grateful to you, Morag Og."

"I do my duty," Morag said stolidly. "You'd best keep the lantern. I can find my way with my eyes closed."

"No need." The other sounded pleased. "My escort is here, I see."

"Yes, ma'am. Good-night to you then." Morag bobbed a curtsey, took the lantern, and turned in the other direction.

Sparrow breathed a silent sigh of relief. Morag evidently intended to take the path that marked a faint trail to the kitchen yard and therefore wouldn't pass her, pressed against the wall of the herb garden, and wishing at that instant that she could melt into the stone.

On the skyline two horses, one ridden and the other led, were approaching. The lady in the feathered hat—did she go to bed in it, Sparrow wondered?—stood, her head raised, her profile sharp against the moon. The woman was surely in her thirties, Sparrow decided, though in all honesty it was impossible to tell at that distance and in that light, but the shape under what appeared to be a travelling dress was mature in outline, and the lady held her head with an arrogant self-confidence seldom seen in young girls.

"*Mignon, je suis ici*," she was saying now, going to meet the approaching rider.

"So I see. You must learn to speak English, Aglaë," Simon Adair responded, dismounting.

"It is a tongue for barbarians," she answered. "There is no music in it."

"I don't suppose William Shakespeare would have agreed with you."

"For your Shakespeare I will give you Racine, Molière—"

"Or the Gaelic," he broke in. "Numerous people still use the Gaelic round here. Now that is a tongue full of music."

"You speak it, Simon?" She had moved closer to him. Her feathers were almost tickling his nose, Sparrow saw with indignation.

"Not one word," he said, laughing, "but I can enjoy listening to the sounds. Come, mount up for we've a ride ahead of us. The tavern is a good four miles off."

"So exact. So English."

Her voice was teasing, but she was mounting.

Sparrow stood, wondering bleakly if it were her destiny to stand perpetually by a wall and watch Simon Adair embrace someone else before he too sprang to the saddle.

Then they were riding away, the hoofbeats sharp in the moonlight.

It was growing definitely chilly. Sparrow realised somewhat belatedly that the hem of her dressing gown was soaked with the night dew and her slippers were wringing wet. She folded her arms tightly about herself and went swiftly to the side door. It would be just her bad luck if someone had come round and bolted it again, she thought gloomily, but nobody had, and she had just entered and picked up the book she had originally chosen when steps and voices sounded in the short passage leading to the main hall.

"Be away to your bed now, Morag. All is ready." It was Angus Og instructing his daughter. Morag answered, "Aye, if it goes well, but that depends on Mr. Roe, and I fear he has doubts."

"Which the rest of us haven't," Angus said briskly.

"We cannot force him to it," she objected.

"He knows his duty," was the uncompromising reply.

The footfalls veered and died away. Sparrow counted a shivering fifty and then sped up the stairs. Gaining her room, she uttered a stifled exclamation of relief and then burrowed in the drawer for a fresh nightgown. The other she bundled up with her dressing gown and slippers and thrust into her travelling trunk. Two torn dresses were sufficient. There was no sense in arousing Morag's curiosity with soaking wet nightwear as well.

The fire in the grate had burned low and the bed had cooled. She pulled the blankets high, opened the book, sneezed violently, then settled herself sternly to read, but the words failed to hold her attention and after a few minutes she let the volume drop to the floor and snuggled down further into the cave of blankets, her last conscious thought before she drifted into a broken sleep being the reflection that Adair and Aglaë matched even more neatly than Simon and Sparrow.

In the morning she awoke with streaming nose and eyes

and a general depression of spirits that caused Morag, bringing in the hot water, to exclaim in concern, "Och, but you've a terrible rheum on you! For heaven's sake stay in bed and I'll tell her ladyship."

Probably she didn't want anybody else to catch the chill and so spoil the party, Sparrow thought somewhat unfairly, since the maidservant was clearly genuinely upset for her, but Sparrow had woken in a mood as scratchy as her throat and was inclined to believe the worst of everybody.

Lady Agnes succeeded Morag, holding a veil across her mouth as if Sparrow had suddenly developed leprosy as she said in agitated tones, "The headache you had was the beginning of this. Do you wish for a physician, my dear? We can easily send for—and congestion of the lungs is so very unpleasant."

"It's only a slight cold, Lady Agnes," Sparrow protested. "A day in bed will set it right."

"You must remain in bed until you are perfectly fit again," Lady Agnes said firmly. "You will not wish to miss the ball and the dinner. You do know that it is to be a fancy dress affair?"

"You didn't say—" Sparrow blew her nose vigorously.

"Mr. Roe thought that it might be amusing. We have contrived to inform those guests who live nearby, and my own wardrobe will supply the deficiency for those ladies who have no costumes."

Fancy dress meant masks and dominoes and ample opportunity for the uninvited to mingle with the legitimate guests. Sparrow looked doubtfully at Lady Agnes, wondering whether that kind lady had thought of that possibility. She reckoned not, and anyway they would have accepted the tutor's suggestion whatever their own opinions.

It was as if they were bound to do Mr. Roe's bidding, as if he were employing them instead of them employing him, as if he held something over them—

Sparrow's alarming train of thought was interrupted by Morag, who bustled in with a bowl of the despised oatmeal liberally sprinkled with salt.

"Sir Alasdair says if you eat all of this you'll be spared worse illness," she announced. Digging in her spoon with a resigned sigh, Sparrow found the hot mealy dish much more tasty and cheering than she had imagined. She ate almost all of it, watched by Morag with arms akimbo, drank a cup of coffee, and was asleep almost before the door had closed behind the maid.

Waking later in the early afternoon she was relieved to discover that her nose had decided to stop dripping and her throat felt less scratchy. Evidently porridge was some kind of miracle cure or, more likely, her own excellent constitution had thrown off the effects of her walk in night clothes and thin slippers.

She plumped up her pillows, noticed that someone had come in at some time and left a jug of lemonade and a bunch of grapes at the side of her bed, and poured herself a tumbler of the fruity liquid. Then she sat back, trying to make sense of the maze in which she had found herself.

The entire village was getting ready to welcome a dead prince. Turn that as she might she could make no sense of it nor fit it into any coherent framework.

Charles Roe was an equal puzzle. A tutor who was positively fawned over by his employers, who had taken— and missed—a potshot at her, who had represented himself to Marie Sinclair as a great-nephew who had died years before—and who was to be kept away from the keep at all costs. Sparrow drained the glass of lemonade and pulled the covers higher. She had no intention of trying to work out what Adam Stuart and Charles Roe had in common, and she had even less intention of racking her brains about Simon Adair's arrival or his connection with the woman called Aglaë. She only knew that it annoyed her exceedingly.

= 10 =

DESPITE THE COMFORTING porridge and the drinks that Morag brought up regularly it was Sunday before Sparrow felt like her old self, and when she rose her legs felt weak and shaky.

"You must not think of coming to church," Lady Agnes said kindly when she presented herself at the breakfast table.

This was not an enormous blow since Sparrow was certain that neither Simon nor the woman called Aglaë would be there either. One more day would see her fully recovered and ready for whatever the birthday celebrations might bring. That they would bring something more than a pleasant dinner and a ball she took for granted. Whether they would bring any absent royalty she regarded as highly doubtful.

It was a fine warm morning with no hint of rain in the breeze. Having promised to wrap up warmly and not to overexert herself, she watched the Stuarts, accompanied by a subdued-looking Mr. Roe, drive off in the open carriage with Angus at the reins, and betook herself to the herb garden with the novel by Mrs. Radcliffe in her hand.

It was a very good novel but it completely failed to hold her attention. The heroine in it was staying in a castle in Italy where there were dungeons and a gorillalike guard who had the uncomfortable habit of following her about. Moreover she was an heiress.

Sparrow, rather wistfully acknowledging the fact that she wasn't an heiress, also reflected that the large, comfortably furnished house and the cordial manners of the Stuarts

146

rendered her own situation very different. Yet there was a puzzle to be solved here and she had the chastening feeling that she wasn't making very much headway.

After luncheon, which was enlivened by Peter's presence and his questions as to how Noah had fitted all the animals in the world into one ark, she excused herself and went upstairs again, Lady Agnes having said in her amiable fashion, "I shall not require your help today, my dear, so you must get as much rest as you can before tomorrow."

"I have not had the opportunity of buying anything to mark the occasion," Sparrow said.

"Nonsense, child," Sir Alasdair looked pleased. "Very sweet thought, but I don't expect gifts at my time of life. Go and rest, and tomorrow I shall claim a dance with you."

Now was the moment for Charles Roe to come up with some gallant phrase but he bent his head, fiddling with his fork, and said nothing. For some reason the tutor was the only one who did not appear to be anticipating the celebrations with any pleasure.

She salved her conscience by lying down for half an hour but the sunshine beyond the window beckoned and she felt increasingly active. Lady Agnes had said that she didn't require her services so there could be no harm in taking a walk. The possibility of being shot at again was to be considered but she decided the risk was small. The marksman, and she was convinced it had been Charles Roe, had evidently intended only to frighten her, and was not likely to make any further attempt. Why he had wished to alarm her in the first place was only another question in the long list of queries she had in her mind.

She put on her cloak and bonnet and took her reticule, though the weight of the pistol was an encumbrance. However, it was better to have it with her, she reckoned, and went softly down the stairs into the main hall. The door to the kitchen was slightly ajar and she could hear Peter's childish treble, "Now, Mrs. Og, do you know how many animals Noah squashed into the ark?"

There was a low, answering murmur. Mrs. Og she had glimpsed briefly once or twice, a tiny woman with greying red hair drawn back into a bun. She looked as if her husband and her daughter had drained her of the vitality that had once been hers, though the meals that came regularly from the kitchen had entailed hours of hard work.

Stepping into the herb garden Sparrow inhaled the mingled perfumes with delight. Bay, mint, tansy, lavender, and rosemary rose into the clear summer afternoon and sprayed their scents like a benediction.

"But you cannot draw back now. We have already wagered too much," Sir Alasdair said.

Sparrow looked round, thinking the laird was close behind her, then realised that his voice had been carried through the partly open window of the library. She stepped hastily out of view of the window but the three people talking within were too intent on their own conversation to consider anything else.

"I am not indifferent to the risks you have chosen to run, but they are greater than you know."

That was Charles Roe, his voice heavy with melancholy.

"My dear sir," Lady Agnes said, an urgent note in her tone, "you cannot refuse to embark upon the enterprise now. All is prepared. The clans are—"

To Sparrow's intense frustration there was the sound of the window being closed and the rest of the sentence was lost. Keeping within the lee of the encircling wall she gained the side door, passed through onto the expanse of unmowed grass, cast a look towards the keep, and then turned in the direction of the moor.

She had gone only a few yards when she saw Lance running towards her, his face wreathed in a grin of relief.

"Cripes, Miss Sparrow, I thought as 'ow you was murdered dead," was his greeting.

"Heavens, what a morbid imagination you have," Sparrow retorted, laughing.

"It weren't imagination," Lance said darkly. "It were common sense. You ain't been seen for three days."

"I caught a cold."

"That's what I 'eard that red-'aired girl tell the minister this morning but I figured that maybe they was poisoning you or 'olding you in a dungeon," he informed her.

"There aren't any dungeons and nobody was poisoning me," Sparrow said crisply, adding, "I'm glad to hear you were in church."

"Not actually 'in,'" Lance said honestly. "More 'anging about behind the gravestones. That girl 'asn't got such a pretty red 'ead as yours is, Miss. Reminds me of carrots, honest to God it does."

"Morag is a very pleasant young woman," Sparrow said severely, "and as you see I am quite safe."

"It wasn't just that." He fell into step beside her as she strolled along the track. "That man 'as turned up again. The one what follows you."

"Simon Adair. Yes, I—"

"Staying at a tavern four miles off," Lance said. "'ired a 'orse and rides about the place after dark—with a lady."

"How do you know all that?" Sparrow enquired.

"The Widow Mackintosh goes to bed early, and when I've 'ad my bit of supper I'm supposed to bed down in the barn, but a barn's the most borin' place you can be in when you ain't very sleepy," Lance said earnestly. "So I walks about and sees what's to be seen. I like walking after dark in these parts. No pickpockets. And I've seen Mr. Adair plain as plain, 'im and 'er.

"She's a looker, she is. But they talk some foreign lingo— Frenchie, I think. I saw 'em over by the big 'ouse the other night, and last night they was in the village, and Mr. Adair says, 'We'd better get back to the Black Prince' in plain English, and that's a tavern four miles off 'cos I asked the Widow Mackintosh."

Sparrow was silent, trying to fit Lance's information into the muddled picture of her own knowledge. Simon and Aglaë were being discreet in their riding expeditions but not so discreet that they could not be seen by anyone abroad after dark. She wondered fleetingly if they were sharing the same room at the Black Prince and frowned so irritably that her companion said in alarm, "Are you mad at me, Miss?"

"No, only at myself," Sparrow said shortly. "I think I have a bad habit of letting my heart rule my head, and then I end up getting the worst of it."

If she hadn't resolved to be noble and renounce Henry and then to save her father's pride and Tizzie's maternal anxiety by lying, and if she hadn't felt sorry for the predicament in which Marie Sinclair was in, she would not now be here at Craig Bothwell under false pretences surrounded by a mystery that, like mist, grew thicker and more puzzling the further she went into it.

"There's something funny going on 'ere," Lance said darkly. "The Widow Mackintosh is in it."

"What's Mrs. Mackintosh got to do with anything?" Sparrow asked.

"She's a bit lacking in the top storey," Lance said. "Very kind but a screw loose somewhere. You ever seen that glove she's got?"

"The one worn by Bonnie Prince Charlie? Yes. Why?"

"She put it in a box yesterday," Lance said, "all tied up with ribbon. She says to me, 'The Prince will be claiming it soon.' I thought as 'ow he was dead."

"He's been dead for a long time," Sparrow assured him. "The Stuart Rebellion ended a long while ago—after the 'Forty—"

"What is it?" Lance gave her an enquiring glance.

"I was going to say after Culloden, when the 'Forty-Five Rebellion was crushed. Lance, you must have some work to do. Run away and do it."

"Are you going to vanish again?" he demanded suspiciously.

"No, of course not—I didn't really vanish," Sparrow said firmly.

"I'll get on then." Lance stuck his hands in the pockets of what looked like a cut-down pair of the late Mr. Mackintosh's trousers and pursed his lips into a whistle.

"I do appreciate the fact that you were worried about

me," Sparrow said. "If I had been poisoned or locked up in a dungeon I would certainly have depended on you to rescue me."

"Would you, Miss?" Lance's face lit up with a broad grin. "Like that cove you was telling me about?"

"The knight, Sir Lancelot? Yes, of course."

"I'll tell you what I think," the boy said. "I think we ought to get on back to London soon as we can. There's that Mr. Adair and 'is lady riding about, and that dead prince fellow coming, and nothing for me to do but milk cows and mend things."

"I intend to leave in a day or two," Sparrow promised, and felt unaccountably lighter of spirits as Lance grinned again and ran off across the moor.

Her own smile faded as she walked on. There were forty-five people going to sit down at the birthday dinner. Forty-six if she counted herself, and hers had been a last-minute invitation. The 'Forty-Five Rebellion was still very clear in Scottish memories. She wondered if the similarity in numbers was merely a coincidence.

She had reached the slope that led up to the kirk and she began to climb it slowly, her thoughts still revolving around the situation that was developing. She had certainly found Marie Sinclair's missing sweetheart even if he wasn't the man he had claimed to be. Even if he wasn't the man he claimed to be. The sentence repeated itself in her mind. Charles Roe was a tutor—had been a tutor for only three months, and before that had been in France and Germany. Fair hair, dark melancholy eyes, and sensitive features. She conjured up her memory of it, seeing the occasionally teasing glint in his expression as if he were aware of something she didn't know and was amused at her ignorance.

"Good afternoon, Sparrow of mine. You are feeling better, are you?"

The enquiry came from beneath the church porch whence Simon Adair now strolled, looking as cool and calm as if there were no mysteries anywhere.

"I do wish," she said sharply, "that you would cease popping up all over the place."

"Well at least you are not balancing on anything now," he said amiably. "You must have a lot of time to spare if you can go a-walking in the middle of the afternoon."

"It does happen to be Sunday," she reminded him, "and I am just now recovered from a very bad cold."

"And I am in the pink of good health," he said with detestable lack of sympathy. "I look forward to seeing you at the ball tomorrow night. I understand fancy dress is to be worn.

"You haven't been invited." She stopped dead and stared at him.

"I am frequently invited to balls," he said. "Did you think me persona non grata everywhere?"

"No, of course not." To her annoyance she found herself blushing slightly. "It is only that you are not acquainted with Sir Alasdair and Lady Agnes, are you?"

"Oh, as we are descended from Adam and Eve," he answered, "then we are all related after a fashion, I suppose. However, I do believe that one of my godmothers knew Sir Alasdair in their youth and naturally asked me to look up the connection since I am staying in the district."

"You would do better to make it a godfather who knew Lady Agnes," Sparrow said. "She is far more vague than the laird."

"Meaning that you don't believe me?" He cocked an eyebrow at her.

"Not one word." It was on the tip of Sparrow's tongue to add that the lady called Aglaë could scarcely invent another godmother in order to scrape acquaintance with the family, but Simon broke in.

"You are too clever for me, Sparrow Harvey. The real truth is that I am a jewel thief who hopes for good pickings when the local gentry flaunt their ancestral wealth."

"So might I be," she retorted. "I am, after all, here on very slight excuse."

"I would like to know exactly why you are here," he said, the mockery dying out of his face. The temptation to confide her doubts and fears to him was suddenly very strong, but some remnant of wariness kept her silent.

"As a temporary companion for Lady Agnes," she said after a moment. "I shall be leaving soon."

"You must let me know when," he returned, unruffled. "I shall take great pleasure in delivering you back to your father."

"Thank you, but I am not a parcel!" She lifted her chin defiantly and found herself encircled by his arms in an embrace that had more fierceness than friendship in it.

"No, you are certainly not a parcel," Simon said, and bent his head, his mouth covering her lips with an urgent passion for which she was completely unprepared. For one instant only her body stiffened and then her lips parted beneath his demanding mouth and she felt long shudders of desire ripple through her own slight frame.

"No!" She was the first to pull back, averting her head. "I have given you no right to believe—you forget that I have only just broken off with Henry."

"Anyone who breaks off with Henry," he returned, "ought to rush immediately into the arms of another partner."

"Meaning yourself, I suppose? No, thank you, Mr. Adair." She freed herself with as much *hauteur* as crimson cheeks and a tumbled bonnet would allow. "I believe that mutual respect and friendship are the twin bases for any lasting relationship. You mustn't fancy that I am unconventional in all my habits."

"What a pity." He was mocking her again. "Respect and friendship are very cool words. For my part I'll start with passionate feeling and let the rest come later."

"Are you," she asked abruptly, "offering me marriage?"

"Good Lord, no!" Mockery was tinged with dismay. "I enjoy my freedom too greatly to be shackled by a pair of apron strings. I was merely—"

"Merely what?"

"Trying to find out something," he answered obliquely.

"Something about me?" Sparrow glowered at him.

"Something about you, but I am not fully answered yet. And here comes the estimable minister to ask if you are recovered from your cold. Good afternoon to you, Sparrow Harvey."

He bowed and strode away between the looming headstones, leaving her to stare after him in exasperation.

"Miss Harvey, how good to see you out and about." The Reverend James Laurie was coming to greet her. "Lady Agnes said you had been unwell. Ah, the guests have begun arriving, I see." His gaze had shifted to Simon's retreating figure.

"Reverend Laurie, did Bonnie Prince Charlie ever marry?" Sparrow asked abruptly.

"Yes, indeed." The minister's eyes returned to her. "He wed quite late in life, I believe. The Princess Louise of Stolberg."

"Were there any children?"

"No, unfortunately the marriage was childless and ended in a divorce or legal separation. I am afraid that Prince Charles Edward Stuart degenerated after the defeat at Culloden."

"Did he have any illegitimate children?" Sparrow persisted.

'My dear young—I do believe there was a daughter born—Charlotte something or other. I do wonder why you require to know?"

"Oh, the legend of the Stuart kings is very romantic, don't you agree?" she burbled.

"The legend but not the reality," he said quellingly. "Oh, there are still a few here and there who drink to the king over the water, choosing not to recall that he died a quarter of a century ago. There are even secret societies here and there that meet to sing the old songs and talk of what might have been, but it is all ridiculous in this modern age." He was continuing but she interrupted.

"Had there been legitimate children, then—"

"As there were not, the question is academic," he said. "I have always cautioned my own parishioners against such foolishness. I would be most annoyed if I heard of any of them becoming members of the Sealed Knot or —"

"The Sealed Knot?" she broke in.

"One of their so-called secret societies," he said. "The White Rose Society is another of them. Quite illegal even though they are completely ineffective. In these modern times we must stand together against the pretensions of Bonaparte, not seek to restore a line that was star-crossed from the beginning. Well, I must not delay you any longer. After a chill it is unwise to linger in the open air too late in the day."

He lifted his shovel hat and turned away, leaving her in a state of excitement almost as overwhelming as that occasioned by Simon's embrace.

The bow with its ends tucked back was a sealed knot, symbol of one of the forbidden Stuart societies. The garden was laid out in that pattern as a sign to those who knew that the Stuarts were loyal to their royal namesakes. The handkerchief in which Marie Sinclair had wrapped the money bore the same symbol. Possibly Charles Roe had given it to her when he was pretending to be Adam Stuart. And Simon had seen it and recognised it too. That was why he was in Scotland. The celebrations for Sir Alasdair's birthday concealed something more sinister—another rising to sweep the Stuarts back upon the throne. And when better than now with the poor king declared insane and a Regency established?

New ideas were crowding into her mind. She sat down on the edge of a nearby tombstone and tried to place them in some kind of coherent order. The bonnie prince who had fled back to France after the defeat at Culloden had died without legitimate issue but there had been a daughter. Named Charlotte, Sparrow reminded herself. But if the daughter were returning to rally the clans for another rebellion then she might also call herself Aglaë. The trouble was that Sparrow had no notion if Charlotte were still alive or how old she would be if she were. The Widow Mackintosh had been expecting a prince. And she had not seemed incurably demented, merely a trifle eccentric and muddled.

The longer Sparrow puzzled, the more the puzzle snarled and tangled in her mind. And the old stone of the slab on which she was perched was sending chills through her skirt. She rose and made her way rapidly back to the house.

Approaching it, looking up at its facade with the window-panes gleaming and smoke puffing cosily from the many chimneys, she found it hard to believe that some treasonous plot was being hatched under its hospitable roof. But someone had taken a shot at her, Charles Roe was not the Adam Stuart he had claimed to be, and Simon and the lady in the hat had a habit of turning up in the most unlikely places.

"Ah, my dear!" Lady Agnes waved to her from the head of the staircase as she went in. "I have a most charming dress for you to wear at the party tomorrow. It needs turning up at the hem but for the rest it will fit you perfectly, I am sure. Come and try it on."

"I had not expected—I mean I have a dress—" Sparrow began protestingly.

"A very charming one, I am sure," Lady Agnes fluttered, "but modern, my dear Sparrow. The hoops and panniers of my younger days were so feminine and graceful."

Her voice was so wistful that Sparrow resolved to hold her peace. And if she were to be a part of the festivities then she might as well dress up, she told herself sensibly, and allowed Lady Agnes to lead the way to the large bedchamber where she could avoid her husband's snoring and dream peacefully of a more leisurely, gracious age.

A gown of pale green silk with a hooped skirt looped up with darker green leaves was laid out on the bed. Next to it padded panniers stood up by themselves.

"I wore this when I attended my coming-out ball when I met Sir Alasdair," Lady Agnes said.

"It's very pretty," Sparrow said sincerely.

"Oh, I was a very pretty young woman," the other said. "Not sparkling, but with good features and a clear skin. Sir Alasdair thought me very charming, anyway, since he offered for me before the season was out. Not that it was a very grand season for we were still mourning the failure of the 'Forty-Five. Fifteen years had passed but people still felt the irony of celebrating anything when the Cause was lost."

"Was it lost, Lady Agnes?" Sparrow asked abruptly. "Was it really lost and broken for ever? I have heard differently."

"One hears so many rumours, my dear." Lady Agnes said vaguely, her eyes clouding. "It is always a mistake to listen to rumour. Now slip off your dress and we will see if this fits neatly."

Obediently Sparrow began to disrobe, wondering if it was foolish to submit to the other's sentimental whim, for it was obvious that Lady Agnes saw herself still as a young girl in the green gown, captivating the dashing Laird of Craigsmuir.

"A little tightening at the waist, I think," was her verdict when the dress was on, the full skirts spread out over the pads. "And your hair must be powdered. We always had our hair pomaded and dressed high."

Sparrow reserved comment, though privately she vowed to try to avoid the powdering. Her own auburn curls looked quite well enough, as she glanced critically into the mirror.

"You are being very kind, Lady Agnes," she felt constrained to say. "I doubt if many companions are treated so."

"The truth is that I don't really need a companion at all," Lady Agnes confided, "though I do plead guilty to a little absentmindedness from time to time. But I do miss female company. Oh, Morag is a dear, good girl and there are some excellent women in the village, but they have their own families, you see, and very soon Peter will be going away to school. I would have loved a daughter, you see. Daughters must be such a comfort."

"I hope my father would echo your sentiments, ma'am," Sparrow said. "I fear he finds me a sad trial sometimes."

"I am sure he does not," Lady Agnes said. "You may tell him that I shall be sorry to part from you when Miss Marchmont recovers. However, I am sure she is a gentlewoman who will share some of my own interests."

She was looking at Sparrow with a faintly questioning air. The latter said hastily, "Is the skirt not a trifle too short, ma'am? It scarcely reaches the ankle."

"Oh, in my day we were not ashamed to reveal a pretty ankle," Lady Agnes said coyly. "Why, my mother went to several of the balls that were given for Bonnie Prince Charlie when he was in Edinburgh and the ladies wore their gowns quite high, above the instep."

"Did you know that the Widow Mackintosh has a glove that belonged to the Prince?" Sparrow asked.

"A wonderful souvenir of her mother's meeting with him, my dear."

"Mrs. Mackintosh is waiting for him to return and claim it."

"She gets a trifle muddled in the head sometimes."

"But he left a daughter, did he not? Charlotte?"

"By Clementina Walkinshaw," Lady Agnes nodded. "She died not long after her father."

"Oh." Sparrow's carefully structured theory came crashing down.

"Perhaps not powder," Lady Agnes said, putting her head consideringly to one side. "That particular shade of red is very charming. The colour of a copper beech."

"I shall be very glad not to be obliged to wear powder, ma'am," Sparrow said thankfully.

"And Mr. Roe did pass a most complimentary remark on it only the other day."

"Lady Agnes, who is Mr. Roe?" Sparrow said bluntly.

"Why, the tutor, my dear. In a temporary position like yourself since Peter will shortly be going away to school. No jewellery, I think. Fresh young beauty needs no adornment. Now, if you will take it off then Morag shall take it in a trifle more at the waist. You have such a small waist that it is a crying pity these ugly modern fashions don't emphasise it."

If Lady Agnes had information she was not prepared to divulge it. Sparrow submitted to being helped out of the dress and drew her own garments over her head again.

"Is there anything I can help you with?" she asked politely.

"Let me see." Lady Agnes thought. "The guests who are to be accommodated in the village will be arriving tomorrow, and our own personal guests a little later—hopefully in time for dinner since Mrs. Og becomes very agitated if her cooking is spoiled. We are to have finnan haddie soup, an *entrée* of veal, neaps with haggis, and a main dish of venison with side dishes of vegetables, and then cloudberries with liqueur cream, oatcakes, and one of Mrs. Og's suet puddings—nothing too heavy and elaborate."

"I already did the menus," Sparrow reminded her.

"So you did. Then there is not very much. You still look a trifle pale after your chill, so I would advise an early night. I intend to have one myself. So many people coming all at once after months, years of quietness. You might care to go up into the attic and see if you can find some suitable bits and bobs for those ladies who have no fancy dress to wear."

The attics stretched over both wings of the second storey and were uncharted territory for Sparrow. She had scarcely set foot on the lowest step of the narrow staircase leading to them when Peter came running up.

"Mr. Roe says I am to amuse myself," he announced. "Can I come with you?"

"May, not can, and yes, you may," Sparrow said pedantically. "We can look for cloaks and feathers and things for the ladies to dress up in."

"It is going to be an excellent party," the little boy chattered as they mounted the stairs and emerged into the first of a series of low-ceilinged rooms connected by arches. Apart from the inevitable dustiness the chambers were reasonably clean, with sufficient light coming through the tiny windows to illumine the boxes and bags and discarded pieces of furniture stacked against the walls.

"I know where Aunt Agnes keeps all her bits and pieces," Peter volunteered. "When I was a child we used to play dressing-up games here. A great many people are coming, aren't they? Mr. Roe is very nervous about it."

"Surely not."

"Very nervous," Peter repeated firmly. "He has been nervous for days, forgetting what he set me as an exercise, walking up and down and frowning mightily. Yes, he does not enjoy birthdays, I think."

"Well, I like them very much," Sparrow said firmly. "I shall enjoy the dinner."

"I was going to be allowed to sit up at table for that," Peter said, his voice somewhat muffled as he dived into a large trunk and pulled out several swathes of brilliantly coloured material. "But the numbers came out wrong because you were given a place, so I will be able to eat with Morag in the kitchen."

"I am very sorry to deprive you of a place," Sparrow began.

"Oh, I like it much better in the kitchen," he assured her cheerfully. "I hate sitting still for long periods. And I shall wear the kilt, you know. The Atholl Stuart tartan since we are a sept of that clan. Mr. Roe will wear—"

"Will wear what?" Sparrow asked, for the child had stopped abruptly.

"I don't think anyone is allowed to know yet," he said at last, "but I saw him trying it on in his room. I went along there to show him a drawing I had made and the door was ajar. He was trying on a kilt. Royal Stuart tartan."

"But I thought only members of the royal—" Sparrow too stopped dead.

"I knew it was the royal tartan," Peter said. "Uncle Alasdair has a book with all the tartans in it. I came away without knocking."

"Why?" Sparrow enquired with interest.

"Mr. Roe looked so miserable," Peter said simply. "He was looking at himself in the glass, and then he sat down and covered his face with his hands. So I came away."

Sparrow forced herself to say casually, "Not every gentleman can wear the kilt successfully. Now here are some feather fans. We shall take those down too."

And she knew who Charles Roe was. Or had to be if her mind was working out the problem logically.

=== 11 ===

ONLY A MEMBER of the royal family had the right to wear the royal Stuart tartan. Sparrow recalled the fury of one newspaper with Jacobite sympathies when the Prince of Wales had worn a tartan waistcoat at some military review or other, its editor complaining that only the exiled Stuarts had the true right to wear it. Her father had pointed out that it was a little unfair since the Hanoverians had Stuart blood too.

"About a teaspoonful, but Prinny would look an ass whatever he wore," Justin had growled.

Bonnie Prince Charlie had died and so had his daughter, but there must be children of hers waiting to reclaim the lost throne.

The only drawback to her theory was that Charlotte had been illegitimate. Or perhaps not? Perhaps there had been a secret marriage such as Charles II had had with Lucy Walter? The son of that marriage, Monmouth, had tried to claim the throne and had been caught and executed for his pains, but there was still doubt as to whether or not there was a marriage licence somewhere that proved his legitimacy. It was too late for Milord Monmouth, who had been executed a century and a half before, but there might still be a legitimate heir to the Stuart crown.

The Sealed Knot, the forty-five invited to sit down at dinner, the keep prepared for the reception of a king, the secrecy that ran like a thin dark ribbon through the sunny fabric of life at Craig Bothwell—all pointed towards a new Jacobite conspiracy.

There was, perhaps, one person who would tell her.

Sparrow pulled on her cloak and went swiftly down the corridor past the half-open door of the bedroom where Lady Agnes and Peter wcrc happily sorting out the various treasures taken from the attic. She hurried across the hall and through the main door and went as fast as her narrow skirts would allow down the drive and onto the bridle path that veered away from the main road towards the village and the moor.

There was no sign of Lance, but as she neared the tiny cottage the Widow Mackintosh came out of the door and squinted towards her, shading her eyes from the long rays of the late sun.

"Miss Sparrow Harvey. The name I recall and also the pretty face," she said cordially. "I hope you've come to take a dish of tea with me."

"With a nip of whiskey to celebrate the occasion," Sparrow said, smiling as she went forward.

"Oh, are we celebrating something today then?" The elderly woman gave her a questioning look.

"Tomorrow, really," Sparrow corrected, "but I am invited to the dinner tomorrow, to make one of the forty-five."

"You know then?" Mrs. Mackintosh stopped as she ushered the younger woman over the threshold.

"Not completely," Sparrow said truthfully. "The Prince married his lady love, didn't he?"

It was a complete shot in the dark but it found its target. Mrs. Mackintosh's face glowed with pleasure and relief.

"My own mother's cousin," she said. "Clementina Walkinshaw. As good and pure a girl as you could find in all of Edinburgh. His Royal Highness met her when he came back to Scotland to claim the throne for his father, King James III. Oh, she fell in love with him and he with her and they were secretly wed. Then he rode away to begin the long march south to London, but he was betrayed and advised to turn back. He stood and fought at Culloden but Butcher Cumberland was there to mow down the clans like wheat. Seven years later the Prince sent for her. They never revealed their marriage, for it was expected that he'd take a royal bride, and they say that soured the love between them, but there was a daughter born."

"Charlotte," Sparrow said, accepting a mug of black, steaming tea into which the good lady had poured a fair amount of whiskey.

"Princess Charlotte, Duchess of Albany," the other corrected. "She wed a gentleman who had been in holy orders—a cardinal no less—Cardinal Roehanstart."

"Charles Roe is their son," Sparrow breathed.

"He is King Charles III of the royal line of Stuart," Mrs. Mackintosh said proudly. "He is his own grandfather come again to set all right after the tragedy of Culloden. Tomorrow he will proclaim himself king and the Jacobites will march again. This time they will not fail."

Carried away by her own eloquence she raised her mug, saying defiantly, "To the king over the water who has come back to his own kingdom."

"The king over the water," Sparrow echoed, slightly carried away herself.

"The clans will gather," Mrs. Mackintosh said, "and the ancient wrongs will be righted."

"Yes," Sparrow said, but her tone suddenly lacked conviction.

"If all goes well," Mrs. Mackintosh said, solemn in her turn. "We have known for some time that a traitor, a government spy, might be among us. Oh, my neighbours never admit me into their confidence but I have heard the rumour. There will be someone at the celebrations who is a false friend. We are ready for that person."

"What will happen?"

"He will be dealt with as all traitors are dealt with," the other promised.

"Oh," said Sparrow, and took another large gulp of the tea.

In her mind flashed the entirely unwelcome picture of the gathered clans dragging Simon Adair to some makeshift scaffold.

"And I must get on," Mrs. Mackintosh said. "It will be too dusky soon to find your way home safely. I take it that you and the Prince—?"

"I beg your pardon?"

"It wouldn't be the first time a member of the royal line has wed a commoner, though if you'll excuse my bluntness we'd have chosen a good Scots lass for him. However, who can command the heart?"

"Who indeed?" Sparrow said, somewhat gloomily as she took her leave. Her suspicions had proved true, though she was a trifle ashamed of the manner in which she had tricked the poor, slightly muddled woman into revealing the whole story, and even more discomposed by the thought that had led Simon Adair and his partner right to the next candidate for the Stuart throne.

For her the whole legend of the ill-starred family had seemed like some remote and ancient tale, and she would never have guessed that another Stuart would arise to make another bid for the throne his forebears had lost.

It was clear that the grandson of Bonnie Prince Charlie had visited London incognito, using the name of a deceased member of the family who were to be his hosts, and then he had met the pretty Marie Sinclair and been compelled to desert her lest she prove unsympathetic to his aims. He had put his royalty above his personal desires. Thinking of that Sparrow felt a wave of sympathy. It was, as Tizzie would have said, beautifully sad.

Mrs. Mackintosh's comments about herself and Charles Roe—she found it hard to think of him as His Majesty King Charles III—were certainly unjustified, though when she thought back she recalled his flirtatious manner, his insistence that she join them at dinner—and the shot that someone had taken at her. She had assumed that Charles Roe had fired. Now she was beginning to think that the shot had not been aimed at her at all. It was just possible that Simon had alighted from the coach a few seconds sooner than he had made out, and that Charles Roe had actually been aiming at him. She wished she could remember every detail of the incident, but it had blurred in her mind.

Simon's following her had had nothing to do with romance. He was obviously the government agent they were expecting. All his actions bore that out. It was unutterably depressing.

She had reached the bridle path and the trees made twisted black shadows against the turf. The sun blazed its last scarlet in the west and over the keep a thin crescent of moon struggled into the sky. At any other time she would have paused to admire the beauty of the scene but now she paused to catch her breath and try to decide what to do. Jacobite societies were officially banned, and Jacobite rebellions, no matter how romantic the cause, were treason. Sparrow felt a nasty little trickle of fear beginning at the base of her spine and shivering upwards. They would all be hanged or imprisoned if she kept silent and, if she spoke out, then Simon would be dragged off and probably hanged too. This was, after all, north of the border, where primitive emotions were still close to the surface. Much as Simon Adair irritated her she felt quite ill at the thought of his meeting a violent end. The lady in the feathered hat could, she thought coldly, take care of herself.

Meanwhile there was nothing for her to do but go back to the house, having formed the resolution that somehow or other, when Simon arrived, she must take pains to warn him that the presence of a spy was known and that he was in imminent danger of discovery.

Someone was watching her. She spun about, her heart jumping into her mouth, as a cloaked figure stepped from the deep shadows beneath the trees.

"Miss Harvey? Oh, I am so very pleased that it is you." The soft voice the brown ringlets and pleading gaze were not frightening, only entirely startling.

"Miss Sinclair, what on earth—? How did you get here?" Sparrow said in astonishment.

"On the stagecoach," Marie Sinclair said. "I received your letter and travelled here at once."

"But you said that you were constrained to remain in London because—"

"I ran away," Marie Sinclair said blandly. "I left a note saying that I was going to stay with a friend. I had to know—how Adam feels about me. I could not endure to wait one more day, you see."

"His name is not Adam Stuart," Sparrow began.

"He is calling himself—"

"Charles Roe. I told you in my letter that he is here as a tutor, save that he is not."

"Not what?" Marie Sinclair said.

"Not exactly a tutor," Sparrow said. "Oh dear, this is all very difficult. You have chosen the worst possible time to arrive."

"He has fallen in love with someone else,," Marie Sinclair said in muted accents and put out her hand imploringly. "Only tell me at once and I shall endeavor to bear it. I shall go away with some of my pride, some of my self-respect intact."

"No, he has not—at least I am not aware of his affections being elsewhere engaged—" Sparrow said hurriedly, feeling a pang of guilt as she recalled his gallantries to herself. "He is not Adam Stuart and neither is he Charles Roe—save that in a way he is, since Roe is the first part of his name—but he is not as he represented himself. Oh, why did you have to come?"

"Miss Harvey, you are not making sense," the other said in bewilderment.

"I know. I am not even making much sense to myself," Sparrow said wryly. "Where have you been staying?"

"At the Black Prince," Marie Sinclair said. "I registered under the name of Mary Smith. I didn't want him to find out that I was in the neighbourhood before I had collected my wits and told him exactly how I feel. But this evening I hired a horse and rode over, just to look at the house, hoping he might emerge for a stroll."

"Is there a dark-haired gentleman staying at the Black Prince called Simon Adair?"

"Yes, I believe so. He is with a very handsome lady somewhat older than—"

"Never mind, I don't wish to hear," Sparrow interrupted. "Miss Sinclair, if you had stayed in London then I would have told you as much as I could upon my return but as it is—"

"Something terrible has happened," Marie Sinclair said. "I can feel it like a weight on my heart. Tell me. I shall be very calm."

"Nothing terrible has happened—yet," Sparrow said hastily, trying to clear her head. "I assure you that he—your friend is safe and well, but he is not a nephew of the family and he is not a tutor, not a genuine one, that is."

"If you are trying to make me believe that he is an—an adventurer," Marie Sinclair said with faltering dignity, "then I shall not cease to love him. If necessary I shall reform him."

She really was remarkably silly, Sparrow thought critically. Nobody ever really reformed the men they loved, else her father wouldn't now be deeply in debt.

"He is a kind of adventurer," she said slowly, "but for very noble reasons. He is—it is not my place to tell you but—"

"Please don't keep me in suspense," Marie Sinclair begged, her voice threatening tears.

"He is named Charles Roehanstart," Sparrow said, yielding to the entreaty.

"Who?'" Marie Sinclair asked blankly.

"The handkerchief in which you wrapped the money you left for me at the stage post—was it yours?"

"No, it was one of Adam's—Charles Roe's. Why?"

"The motif embroidered in one corner is the sign of a secret Jacobite society."

"I don't see what—are you telling me that he has some connection with an illegal society?"

"He is the grandson of Bonnie Prince Charlie," Sparrow said, giving in completely. "His mother was the prince's legitimate daughter."

"Then that makes him the rightful king of England," Marie Sinclair said after a short pause.

"If you're a person with Jacobite sympathies."

"Now I understand." The other girl gave a quivering little laugh. "He was in London incognito, to seek out supporters perhaps, and when we met—a monarch could not possibly marry an ordinary girl like myself."

"He isn't a monarch yet," Sparrow said sensibly. "And his grandfather secretly married a very ordinary girl from Edinburgh."

"Secretly?"

"He was expected to marry a princess," Sparrow admitted reluctantly.

"So he left me," Marie Sinclair said desolately. "Now I understand why he never replied to my letters. He knew that it was useless to pursue the relationship between us."

"If that was his reason then I don't think much of it," Sparrow said stoutly.

"His first duty was to the Cause." Marie Sinclair gave a miserable little sob. "I fear that I have put you to a lot of inconvenience."

"For which you paid me far too much money," Sparrow said. "If I were not in need of it I would offer to give it back to you. What are you going to do now?"

"Go back to London," Marie Sinclair said dismally. "I shall not embarrass him by advertising my presence."

"But we don't really know for certain," Sparrow said, struck by an idea, "if he actually got your letters. Perhaps Sir Alasdair or Lady Agnes confiscated them without telling him."

"Why should they do that?" the other demanded.

"Perhaps they don't want him to have any romantic connections with anyone from England."

"Do you think that's possible?" There was a note of hope in the soft voice. "Oh, if I could only believe that his was not a deliberate desertion."

"On the other hand he hasn't written to you."

"I said that I would write first. If he never received my letter then he may imagine that I was merely indulging in a flirtation," Marie Sinclair said eagerly. "Oh, if I could but see him, speak to him—"

"Tomorrow there is a celebration here, to mark Sir Alasdair's seventy-fifth birthday," Sparrow said thoughtfully, "though I think the party has another purpose. However, there are going to be more than a hundred people coming, and it is fancy dress, masks, and dominoes. You might mingle with the guests and find some opportunity—"

"I will venture it. Oh, you have no notion what a relief it is to have such a sensible friend," Marie Sinclair said softly.

Sparrow would have disclaimed the compliment, but the other pressed her hand fervently and glided back into the shadows. The jangle of harness and the sound of hoofbeats muffled by the turf signalled her departure.

Marie Sinclair's sudden advent was another complication. It was plain that Charles Roe had either decided to end the affair or others were intervening to keep him and Marie apart. Sparrow reflected on the silliness of young women who, fancying themselves in love, threw caution to the winds and hared up to Scotland to find out what was going on.

She had reached the side door when she saw the very gentleman she had been thinking about seated behind the uncurtained window of the library, his head bent over a volume. Her step on the path must have alerted him for he rose at once and came to open the door for her.

"You have missed your dinner, I fear," he said. "The meal was served early because the party tomorrow is going to take up people's time. Morag will have something for you in the kitchen, I daresay. Have you had a pleasant walk?"

"Pleasant enough." She wondered what he would say if she informed him that she had just been talking to the sweetheart he had left behind in London. Perhaps he would be happy to learn that she was in the district or embarrassed because he had no intention of seeing her again.

"Tomorrow is a big day," he said. "So many guests expected."

"That's true." Sparrow regarded him with some sympathy. The following day would, she was convinced, mark his proclamation as the heir to the throne. She wondered how he really felt about his situation, how she would feel were she in his place.

"I shall be looking forward to dancing with you," he said. "You must have realised that your loveliness has had a most profound effect upon my susceptibilities."

"My—?" Sparrow stared at him.

"And your modesty," he went on. "You are not aware of the effect you have, perhaps?"

"I think I will go and ask Morag for something to eat," Sparrow said hastily, but he had risen and stood between her and the inner door.

"You think that I am flirting?" he said. "You think that a mere tutor would not presume to use such language to a young lady who, for some reason private to herself, chooses to take a post as companion?"

"There's nothing private about my reason," Sparrow interrupted. "I needed the money."

"And you expect me to believe that is the sole reason? Come, your dresses and your manners mark you out as someone higher in station than the general run of paid companions," he said.

She toyed briefly with the idea of telling him that she was a princess in disguise, but that was too near the truth to be allowable.

"Women who earn their living are frequently well educated and decently attired," she said instead.

"And seldom lovely. Beautiful women are usually married."

"I am not yet of age," she said primly. "Now, if you will excuse me, sir—"

"Sparrow, if I may call you so, don't run away," he said with his slight and charming smile.

"I can't run anywhere," she pointed out crisply, "since you are standing in the way."

"I find it difficult to believe," he persisted, "that you are no more than you say you are. That you came here—"

"As a substitute for Miss Marchmont. That is exactly what I am, Mr. Roe. Now, am I to stand here and starve to death or will you let me by?" Sparrow demanded, half laughing, though her cheeks were flushed with annoyance.

"On payment of a forfeit," he said teasingly.

"I have noth—"

"A kiss—upon the hand? You cannot object to that surely?"

She stuck out her hand, allowed him to place a too-lingering salute on her fingers, then swiftly gained the inner door.

"You think me too bold, Miss Sparrow? My manners are not pleasing to you? On the Continent I am accounted something of a ladies' man."

"I'm sure you are," Sparrow said crossly, "but we are in Scotland now, Mr. Roe."

"As I am reminded every morning when that wretched oatmeal is served," he said ruefully. "I go quite cold when I think of eating it every day for the rest of my life."

"You will stay on here then after Peter has gone to school?' she enquired artlessly.

"There are considerations of duty." His face was mournful again. Then he smiled, as if he had dismissed something from his mind. "Well, go and eat some dinner. And don't be offended at the admiration I pay you. It is only my manner."

But admiration from the wrong man for the wrong girl was worse than no admiration at all. Sparrow went through to the kitchen where she found Morag, who put down her knitting and rose at once to bring soup and cold meat.

"I was just thinking that in ten minutes I'd be sending my father out to look for you, Miss," she said, as she set out the dishes at the end of the scrubbed oaken table. "Will it bother you to eat here? I can set up in the solar for you."

"Here is fine," Sparrow assured her, sitting down and

making eager inroads into the soup.

"The rest of them ate early," Morag explained, taking up her knitting again. "It's to be a big day tomorrow. All the people coming and the music—och, it'll be just grand."

"I believe that some of the guests are already arriving," Sparrow said.

"None of the houseguests yet. There are some staying in the village and there'll be some at the tavern four miles off, I daresay. I suppose it will seem very tame to yourself after the excitements of London."

"London," Sparrow informed her with feeling, "has not half as much excitement as I am finding here."

"Not that Lady Agnes really needs a companion for all that she's a wee bit absentminded," Morag said tolerantly, "but she gets lonely."

"And don't you? Get lonely, I mean."

Morag considered and then shook her head. "I was brought up here," she said. "I would like to see Edinburgh before I die just be able to say that I've been, but Craigsmuir suits me well enough. Mind, it isn't now as it was in the old days before the Stuarts were driven out by the usurper kings, and the clans broken. There are clans who were wiped out more than fifty years back, Miss Sparrow."

"But you don't recall them surely."

"No, of course not, but my father has told me, and Sir Alasdair was here. He was only a lad of ten when Culloden was fought, and he regretted all his life that he was too young to march with Bonnie Prince Charlie's men when they set off south. He used to tell Adam the tales of the old days and how it would be when—but I'm dropping stitches while I chatter. Excuse me."

She bent her gaze to the shining needles again, her mouth a tight line in her plain face. Sparrow wondered what she had been on the point of saying. When the Prince comes into his own again and the clans rise up?

She finished her meal, drained the cup of coffee that Morag had poured, murmured good-night, and made her way to her own room. The lamps had been trimmed and the covers turned back. Sitting down on the end of the bed, Sparrow tried to compose herself.

Charles Roe—it was impossible to think of him as King Charles—was, for all his royal blood, an unmitigated flirt who had deceived poor Marie Sinclair and wouldn't scruple to deceive any other young girl who was foolish enough to believe in his nonsense. She might have been tempted to respond to him herself had she not met Si—had she not made up her mind that there was little happiness to be found in chasing after a husband.

Too much was beginning to happen too rapidly, she thought. The pieces of the puzzle were tumbling into place and the pattern they created was displeasing. Her first act must be to try to warn Simon that the presence of a government agent was suspected, and she had no notion as to how to go about it. She could hardly walk the four miles to the Black Prince, and she could think of no excuse for borrowing a horse to make such a journey.

And when that task was accomplished she had to find some means of bringing Charles face to face with the girl he had deceived and abandoned in London, if he himself were not the one being deceived.

Sparrow gave a deep and heartfelt sigh, thinking wistfully of the two imaginary little boys whom Tizzie thought she was now taking care of. Odd that she should have hit upon the name of Adam for one when there had been an Adam in the family—no, she corrected herself, not odd at all since she had already heard the name of Adam Stuart from Marie Sinclair.

There was no sense in brooding here when she ought to be catching up on her sleep in preparation for the next day. She looked gloomily at the green gown now hanging over the back of a chair. It would have been nice to have worn it and gone to the birthday party with nothing more on her mind than having a sparkling evening.

It was not until she was in bed and just dropping off to

sleep that the voice at the bottom of her mind said clearly, "But it was a lie, don't you see?"

And then she was asleep and the voice in her head was silent.

= 12 =

"IT IS GOING to be a fine day," Lady Agnes said the next morning when Sparrow presented herself at breakfast. "Morag took in your dress at the waist, my dear. I think it will fit you admirably now."

"Thank you, Lady Agnes," Sparrow said, thinking how odd it was that they should be talking about the trivialities of dress when this day was marked out for momentous events.

"I shall decorate the table myself," Lady Agnes was continuing. "Small bowls, I think. There is nothing more irritating than not being able to see one's table companions without darting one's head from side to side to avoid some large centrepiece. What do you think, my dear?"

She addressed her question to Sir Alasdair, who glanced up from his eggs and answered, somewhat shortly, "Put the flowers where you choose. There are more important matters to think about."

"Yes, yes, to be sure." His wife was slightly flustered. "The food and the guest rooms all made ready and—Sparrow, the piper is to come from the village. I think we had better remind him to be on time. Archie Wilson lives in the cottage nearest to the kirk. I shall give you a note for him. There is no need for you to hasten back. Indeed you might take a basket and see if you can find any more of the lilies."

"Yes, ma'am," Sparrow said, silently thanking whatever Providence had inspired Lady Agnes to send her on an

She set off directly after breakfast, taking a small basket and the note for Archie Wilson. Certainly it was a fine, warm morning. The sun, breaking through puffs of white cloud, gilded the moor, and the village looked trim and new as if it were newly built for the occasion.

She delivered her note to a brawny fellow, who received it with the sour comment, "Her ladyship knows full well that I'd as soon lose my pipes as be late tonight of all nights, but she was ever a one for fussing."

"We are all looking forward to it," Sparrow said.

The other's manner became perceptibly more mellow. "You'll have nothing to compare with the reel and the skirl of the pipes in England," he said.

"No, nothing. You have been to England?"

"No thank God," he said piously. "Neither I nor any of my kin."

"It isn't as bad there as all that," Sparrow muttered, nettled, as she took her leave and bent her steps onto the path that wound below the mound on which the church stood towards the moor.

She was fortunate in catching sight of Lance within ten minutes. He came running across the turf towards her, his face lighting with pleasure. Sparrow couldn't help noticing that since his coming into Scotland he looked much cleaner, and the pastiness of his skin had given place to a more healthy glow, but his first words were the inevitable, "Morning, Miss. When are we going 'ome then?"

"Very soon, I expect, though you are free to stay on as long as you like," Sparrow told him.

"It's boring," he grimaced. "Nothing but cows, sheep, and 'eather. What was you wanting?"

"There is a tavern four miles from the village—"

"The Black Prince on the Edinburgh road."

"Would it be possible for you to take a message there?" she enquired. "To Mr. Simon Adair?"

"The gent what's following you? That don't make much sense," he objected.

"Believe me but it makes a great deal of sense though I am not bound to explain it to you," Sparrow said repressively. "Can you take the message? It is of the utmost importance. Mrs. Mackintosh will not—"

"The old lady's getting 'erself toffed up for the party," he said. "She gave me the day off. Said I can do as I like provided I don't get into mischief."

"Then you will take it?" She opened her reticule and brought out the letter she had penned at first light. Its contents were brief and succinct.

> Dear Mr. Adair,
>
> You are suspected and will be discovered unless you leave for London at once.
>
> Your sincere friend,
> Sparrow Harvey

Short and to the point, she had decided, carefully sealing it. She hoped that Simon would have the good sense to take heed.

"Is it true that a prince is coming to take over the throne?" Lance asked, taking the letter.

"Is that what Mrs. Mackintosh says?"

"Been going on about it all morning," Lance informed her. "She's put that glove in some fancy box and she's taking it to the party with 'er tonight. What's wrong with Prinny then? Don't they take a shine to 'im up in Scotland?"

"Not a very great shine," Sparrow said, amused despite herself. "They are loyal to the Stuart kings up here. You will be sure to deliver the note."

"Cross me 'eart and 'ope to die, but not just yet." He gave her one of his cheerful grins and scampered off. Sparrow, looking after him, decided that one good thing at least had come out of her trip to Craigsmuir. Lance was starting to act more like a boy and less like a cringing remnant of the dregs of humanity. It was a pity that he would be returning to the slums that had stunted his growth and made him old before his time.

She reminded herself that she had undertaken to find

more of the tiny white lilies and concentrated on her task, her head bent as she walked since the green turf was broken up by patches of black peat bog that became larger as she moved further from the village. The morning had worn away before her basket was full again and she retraced her steps, glad of the brilliant sunshine which made the way back so easy to ascertain, thinking how frightening it would be to be caught by the haar in this lonesome spot.

It was no use. She was deliberately fixing her mind on nonessentials because she didn't want to think about Simon Adair. There was no doubt in her mind that his only reason for following her was because he believed that she could lead him to the heart of the conspiracy, and his arrival at the ball would herald the arrest of the kindly Stuarts. Or it might result in his own capture by prospective rebels whose only care was to silence him. Sparrow sighed, tripped over a root, let out one of her father's more colourful expletives and, feeling not a whit better for it, marched back towards the house.

Visitors were arriving. There were coaches drawn up in the stable yard and, when she went into the front hall, she could hear the hum of conversation from the drawing-room.

"Her ladyship says that she'll be obliged if you'll finish off the table decorations," Morag said, striding through from the kitchen quarters. "There's to be a light luncheon, a buffet where people can help themselves, and I don't know whether I'm on my head or my heels for all the excitement."

Sparrow went through to the dining-room, where the long table had been fully extended and set with china, silver, and crystal. There were small silver bowls of flowers down the centre of the table but room for the ones she had picked in a larger bowl on the board. Taking off her cloak, she proceeded with her task.

A light footfall attracted her attention and, raising her head, she beheld Charles Roe.

"Do I disturb you?" he enquired.

"No, not at all," she said, her fingers smoothing petals and leaves. "You are not with the guests?"

"I have instructions to remain out of the way until this evening when I shall be sprung upon the company like a—"

"Long-lost prince?" she said.

"Then you know?" To her surprise his mobile face expressed the deepest disappointment.

"That you are grandson to Bonnie Prince Charlie? I would have to be a complete idiot not to have guessed it. The whole neighbourhood awaits your proclamation."

"You guessed it?" He raised his head, looking at her intently. "You were unaware when you first came here?"

"Of course I was unaware," she said in surprise. "I came to act as temporary companion to Lady Agnes. I had no idea that there was tr—"

"Treason brewing? You would call it treason?"

"I wasn't calling it anything," she said crossly. "It has nothing to do with me. I cannot imagine why I am invited to sit down at dinner."

"That was my wish," he reminded her. "You really did not know when you first met me?"

"I told you so." Sparrow bit her lip, wondering if now was the moment to acquaint him with the fact that his abandoned lady love was in the vicinity, but before she could decide whether or not to speak he said, "Then I am immeasurably relieved that my aim was off."

"It was you then who shot at me?"

"I had reason to believe you an informer," he said gravely. "The quickest way with informers is to dispose of them with as little fuss as possible, but when the moment came, just after the stage had passed and you stood unprotected in the road, I could not bring myself to do it. Killing was never in my style, Miss Sparrow, and my own feelings for your person were too warm. I let off a shot to frighten you from over the wall and then fled back to the house."

"You might have killed me!" she cried indignantly.

"Had I wished to kill you be assured the shot would not have gone wide," he said. "No, I hoped that the near accident might cause you to leave."

"Well, you certainly frightened me," she admitted.

"And now you say you had no knowledge—which means that I must look elsewhere." He was silent for a moment, his dark eyes brooding. It was possible now to see his close resemblance to the portraits she had seen of the long-faced Stuart kings with their dark eyes and their sensual mouths and the inherent weakness in their sensitive, inbred features.

"Mr. Roe, I have to tell you—" she began.

"Sir, what in the world are you doing here? It is too early. Indeed it is." Lady Agnes had swept in, consternation on her face. "You are not to appear until dinner. Sir Alasdair was most anxious that all should be done with ceremony. Morag will bring refreshments to your room."

"And after the dinner we shall go to the keep and there make the proclamation? There has been much activity in that old building recently," he said, gently teasing.

"Oh, it was to be a surprise," Lady Agnes said in disappointment. "Everything arranged in formal fashion. My dear Sparrow, this really is nothing to concern you."

"Miss Sparrow knows," he said. "I wished her to sit with us earlier for a different reason, but now she will sit with us as a friend."

He thought me a spy and meant to denounce me, not having the resolution to shoot me himself, Sparrow thought indignantly. She longed to give him a piece of her mind, royalty or no, but Lady Agnes was bustling him through the kitchen quarters again and the moment was lost.

"Well, it is an immense relief that you know," Lady Agnes said, returning almost instantly. "Sir Alasdair was quite miffed with me that I should choose to engage a companion at the very time when plans were being made—but if His Majesty himself vouches for you then all is splendid. Depend upon it, but he admires you very much. It would be

rather marvellous if his approbation were to turn to—
though a Scottish wife would have been more popular. But
royalty cannot be refused."

Oh yes it can, Sparrow thought grimly. Charles Roe or
Roehanstart or King Charles or whatever he called himself
would have to learn that he couldn't run round leaving a
trail of broken hearts behind him, and in the unlikely event
that his mad enterprise succeeded Queen Sparrow sounded
absolutely ridiculous. On the other hand it would be rather
satisfying to put Simon Adair in the Tower of London.

"Is there anything else I can do?" she enquired aloud.

"Everything is being done, dear," Lady Agnes said. "We
have extra help from the village and the Ogs are being
simply marvellous. You delivered the note to Archie
Wilson?"

"Yes, ma'am."

"Though his pipes will scarcely be heard above the
others."

"Others?" Sparrow looked at her.

"The clans, my dear. The summons has gone out. The
clans will be marching over the moors soon to greet their
exiled monarch. Our guests are all chiefs, you see. We sent
out word months ago that the day was coming when the
tartans would be worn and the old loyalties be called upon."

The older woman's eyes were shining and her face was
young with dreaming. With sudden perception Sparrow
saw that this Stuart prince brought with him hopes that
must have died with the gunshot that had killed Adam
Stuart. Peter was only a child, too young for his future
character to give his great-uncle and great-aunt joy, but in
the Cause they could both recapture all the high hopes of
their youth.

"Why now?" Sparrow asked aloud. "Why wait so long?"

"The usurper was not pronounced definitely mad before,"
Lady Agnes said. "The English were content enough with
their Hanoverian monarch, but now it is certain that he is
insane and that the Prince Regent is a fat fool and neither

Scots nor English are happy. It is the perfect moment for the restoration of the Stuarts."

"Of the legitimate line," Sparrow said.

"Exactly." Lady Agnes beamed. "I knew the minute I laid eyes on you that you would be one who sympathised with the Cause. It would not astonish me to discover that you have some Scots blood.'

"Not one drop, I'm afraid," Sparrow said, but the other had gone over to look at the table.'

"Our finest china and silver and the Venetian glassware," she said happily. "All of it was hidden away by my husband's mother after Culloden. That was a terrible time, I believe. So many hanged and transported and so many homes burned down. The keep was almost destroyed by the English on their way south again. That was when this house was built. It took a very long time to build up the family fortunes again, though, and then everything began to go wrong. David's son, Adam, was named for Sir Alasdair's elder brother, you know, the one who fell at Culloden, and then there was the terrible accident and then David married again—and now we have Peter, who is a nice child, but not Adam. He may grow up to resemble Adam, of course, but there's a wee while to wait yet, and Sir Alasdair and I are not growing any younger. Having His Majesty here is almost like having Adam back again, as if he never really died. But you must go and rest, my dear. There is nothing to do now but wait for the clans to come."

And for Simon Adair to turn up, Sparrow thought grimly as she left the room. She had begun to think that sending him a note of warning had been fruitless. Government agents would not be likely to arrive alone in order to arrest more than a hundred traitors. No doubt there were others waiting in the vicinity to move in when he gave the signal.

The great house was humming now with chatter and bustle. Maidservants were taking trays of refreshments into the drawing-room and another group of gentlemen was dismounting at the main door.

Sir Alasdair's voice boomed from the library, "You will have to forget your grudge against the Campbells on this one occasion, my dear sir. Private revenges have no place among us now. I could wish you had brought more men, or do they come later?"

An indeterminate murmur answered him. Sparrow frowned, slowly climbing the stairs. If this was the start of a serious rebellion then they would need more than a few hundred men.

"Miss Harvey!" One of the maids, a mobcap covering her head, was beckoning to her from the upper landing.

"Miss Sinclair, what are you doing here?" Sparrow demanded, hurrying up the last flight.

"I thought this was good way of gaining entrance," Marie Sinclair said. "There are so many coming and going that they will not notice an extra one. I could not endure to wait any longer, Miss Harvey. I must see and speak with him, learn his feelings for me from his own lips. You can understand that, can't you?"

"He will not appear among the company until this evening," Sparrow said, wishing the other elsewhere.

"You have not mentioned me?"

"No, not a word. You said that—"Sparrow hesitated.

"It must be a private interview," Marie Sinclair said. "If he rejects me then I will leave at once. Is there not somewhere we can meet? You know where his room is? Oh, I long to see his face, hear his voice. You cannot imagine, Miss Harvey."

Sparrow could imagine very well the hunger of desire that must grip a woman separated from the man she loved. What she could not imagine, she realised with a jolt, was wrapping some coins in a handkerchief belonging to the said lover and giving the packet casually to a stranger. It was out of character. Sweet, sentimental Marie Sinclair would never have done such a thing. She would have kept the handkerchief as a souvenir laid in rosemary while she waited for the reunion, just as Mrs. Mackintosh's mother had treasured the prince's glove.

And Charles Roe, seeing the handkerchief, had not looked ashamed or guilty as if he were remembering the girl he had abandoned. Instead he had jumped to the conclusion that Sparrow herself was the government agent, sent to hunt him down and betray him. And he had tried to frighten her away by taking a shot at her.

"Is something wrong?" Marie Sinclair whispered.

"I am thinking what is best to be done," Sparrow said in a distracted manner.

"If I could only speak to him—" the other repeated.

"Not here. There are too many people about," Sparrow said. "The keep beyond the herb garden, away from the house, is being prepared for him. You could wait there. It's locked but I can get the key. Then I'll tell him to slip across and talk with you."

"Don't mention that I am here. I want our meeting to be unexpected," Marie Sinclair said.

"I'll think up some excuse to get him there," Sparrow promised. "Go down through the stable yard and I'll follow with the key."

She was immeasurably relieved when the other girl ducked her head and hurried down the stairs again.

Morag kept the key. Sparrow counted to ten and then went down to the kitchen where Mrs. Og was supervising what seemed like an army of helpers.

"Morag." Sparrow intercepted the maidservant, who was carrying a large ham to the chopping board. "Lady Agnes requires the key to the keep. Some surprise or other has been planned."

"Take it and welcome," Morag said promptly. "I never did enjoy the responsibility." She undid the heavy iron key from the bunch jangling at her waist and went back to her chores.

Marie Sinclair was waiting in the shadow of the creeper-clad building, her mobcap pulled forward to obscure her features. She looked nervous and excited.

"You go in," Sparrow advised, "and I'll fetch Mr.—him as quickly as I can. You must give me time though, for I must find him, think of some excuse to bring him here—"

"Not mentioning my name," the other reminded her.

"It shall be a surprise," Sparrow said, turning the key, which slid smoothly in the lock, and standing aside to let her companion enter.

"When I behold his face then I will know his true feelings," Marie Sinclair said.

For a second that lasted about three weeks she stood on the threshold, and then she passed into the lowest storey. Sparrow closed the door and turned the key in the lock softly. It would, with any luck, be a considerable while before Marie Sinclair realised that she was locked in.

She needed that time to think, to tidy up the pattern in her mind. She walked away from the keep, remembering that Miss Sinclair might be checking on her movements from one of the arrow slit windows. It had to look as if she were hurrying to find Charles. Near the wall she veered away towards the bridle path, losing herself among the trees.

Charles had visited London, fallen in love with Marie Sinclair, and then discovered that she was an agent for the government. He had left her abruptly and gone up to Craigsmuir, and Marie Sinclair, aware that she had been found out, had herself found a substitute who could be tricked into looking for a lost lover. It had been careless of her to use the handkerchief in which to tie up the money, or had that been the signal to inform Simon Adair that Sparrow was the one to be followed? And she, Sparrow, had played right into their hands by sending a letter to Marie informing her that the tutor was there and was her missing sweetheart. And then Marie Sinclair and Simon Adair and that befeathered woman who called herself Aglaë had all travelled up together in the stage and they were still using her to lure the grandson of Bonnie Prince Charlie into their clutches.

She wondered briefly why they had not laid hands on him in London, but her reason told her that until he was proclaimed as rightful king, until the clans had gathered, there were no grounds for apprehending him. They planned to seize all the active members of the Sealed Knot Society and bring a final end to the Jacobites. And she had been the one used to further the scheme.

Sparrow was astonished to discover that her eyes were brimming with tears. Not for Charles, who was going to reclaim his ancestors' throne if he could but for her own stupid self. She had really believed in one tiny corner of her heart that Simon Adair liked her, that he might possibly have followed her for romantic reasons, but he was interested only in running the Stuart heir to earth.

Well, she had Marie Sinclair safely locked up until she could decide what to do about her, and she had sent warning to Simon to leave since his activities had been discovered. Now she had better find Charles and tell him what was happening. What she really wanted to do was sit down and howl her eyes out. It was terribly uncomfortable hating someone as much as she hated Simon Adair.

She blinked back the tears resolutely and made her way back to the house just as another carriage drew up. A hired carriage with a bewhiskered driver pulling on the reins, and the door opening to reveal a handsome young man who sprang down lithely, turning to help his companion with a smiling, *"Nous sommes ici, ma belle Aglaë. Viens!"*

The lady was certainly handsome, Sparrow thought, but older than Simon. Definitely very much older. Practically middle-aged. Thirty-three if she was a day.

As they went up the shallow steps and through the main door together, Sparrow stood stock-still in the drive and decided furiously that it would be entirely Simon Adair's own fault if he ended the evening by getting shot. For two pins she was near doing it herself.

= 13 =

"THERE YOU ARE, my dear." Lady Agnes rustled down the stairs as Sparrow went slowly in. "I am all of a dither with so many guests at once. Can you amuse Peter for a while? He is to wear the kilt tonight and be allowed to watch the dancing for a while. You look quite discomposed. I hope your cold is not returning?"

"No, I feel quite well," Sparrow hastened to assure her. "Is Mr. Roe not taking care of Peter?"

"It would hardly be fitting now," Lady Agnes said with faint reproof. "He is writing his speech of acceptance."

Acceptance of a throne now firmly in Hanoverian hands, Sparrow thought. Climbing the stairs she kept her eyes open for any sign of Simon or his companion, but whatever tale they had told had obviously gained them entry and, no doubt, they were now mingling with the other guests in the drawing-room. She paused at the head of the stairs to scowl down at the closed doors and then turned in the direction of the schoolroom.

Peter, already clad in kilt and sporran with a tiny dagger stuck proudly into his stocking and a lace jabot on his shirt greeted her more boisterously than usual. "When may I go down to join the company?" he demanded. "Aunt Agnes says they will not relish a small boy running round, but I could be a great help in handing round cakes and things. Mr. Roe is writing a speech. Did you know that he is not Mr. Roe at all, but the king from over the water?"

"The call has gone out to the clans," he went on excitedly. "They will gather here and then march south. They will win this time because the English are too busy with the French to have time to look towards Scotland."

He was obviously quoting something he had heard his elders say. For a moment Sparrow felt a ripple of excitement herself. Then she recalled that this Jacobite rebellion was not even likely to begin since one government agent was locked up in the keep and two more had actually gained access to Craig Bothwell.

"Let me hear you say your poem," she suggested. "Then we will play a game of spillikins until it is time for me to go and change."

The prospect didn't grip him with any very great enthusiasm but he obediently recited his poem with many gestures and settled reluctantly to spillikins. He won easily because his partner was paying very little attention to the game. Marie Sinclair must have realised by now that Charles wasn't hastening to the keep. What, Sparrow wondered, would she do? She could scarcely yell for help from the windows without revealing her identity, and as Sparrow herself had the key nobody else was likely to enter the old building. Meanwhile, the erstwhile tutor was composing his speech of acceptance, Simon and that woman were by now firmly ensconced as bona fide guests, the clans were expected, and she was playing spillikins with a child who looked upon the whole day as a brave adventure without realising that before it was over there must surely be a violent outcome.

"Come along, Peter." Morag tapped at the door and entered. "Her ladyship is giving out fans and cloaks and masks to the ladies who didn't bring any and you may come to help. Miss, I put everything ready in your room. Dinner's an hour early."

Sparrow went docilely along to her own room. There was no point in her trying to do anything at the moment. When she saw Simon she would contrive to warn him that the presence of a spy was known. Meanwhile she might as well make herself as pretty as possible though it was doubtful if Si—if anyone would notice.

A narrow silver mask had been added to the green dress over the back of the chair. Tying the panniers about her waist and wriggling into the dress she snatched a look at herself in the mirror and was pleased by the charm of the slight figure she beheld. The dress was vastly becoming and the lack of hair powder was an advantage rather than otherwise since the pale green flounces suited her flame-coloured curls and the mask gave her a piquant air.

The house was humming with activity. When she opened her door she could hear laughter and chatter, and then Lady Agnes went past in a gown of gold brocade with her white hair piled so high that it was fortunate the doors were also high.

"I am," Sparrow thought miserably, "on a cleft stick." To denounce Simon might bring about the very violence she feared but to allow the intended proclamation to continue would mean exposing the kindly Stuarts to a charge of treason. Sparrow wasn't sure if any criminals were still beheaded, but she was certain equally unpleasant fates were meted out to them. Her one slight hope was to find Charles and warn him that his course of action would bring his prospective subjects into grave danger. She doubted if he would listen but at that moment she couldn't summon up any more brilliant idea.

Accordingly, she turned and went into the other wing, hoping that she would hit on the right room where Charles was even now finishing off his speech.

She might have passed by it altogether but the sound of voices from within a chamber at the end of the corridor alerted her attention. The words were too muffled to distinguish, but she could recognise the smooth tones of the prospective king.

Tapping politely, she heard a sudden silence. Then his voice was raised, "Yes?"

"It's Sparrow Harvey," she raised her voice to say. "I have to talk with you."

A moment's pause was succeeded by an invitation to enter. The bedroom was far more luxurious than would have been given to any genuine tutor. Her whole attention, however, was centred on the fair-haired man who leaned back in the easy chair he was occupying and said, "Even masked your beauty blinds me, Miss Sparrow."

"You are going to be proclaimed as king this evening, aren't you?" Sparrow said breathlessly, "and then the clans will march into England and there will be bloodshed and you cannot win. There are government agents all over the place—and the instant you are acknowledged as monarch the Stuarts will be arrested, or the agents may be killed, and whatever happens it will all be absolutely dreadful."

She ceased talking, fixing her eyes beseechingly on him.

"What do you think?" Charles said. He spoke not to her but to someone standing behind her in the window recess.

As she swung round, Simon, clad immaculately in evening dress, stepped forward, answering, "You will have to pardon my friend. She is not really astray in her wits though she often behaves as if she were."

"I thought you—" Sparrow stopped, her mouth falling open foolishly. "I don't—Mr. Roe, sir, this gentleman—" She stopped again.

"Is assuredly not a government agent," Simon said amiably. "Is that what you have been fancying about me? Rather odd, really, when for some time I thought exactly the same thing about you."

"That," said Sparrow, with as much dignity as she could muster, "is absolute nonsense."

"Were you on your way to denounce me?" Simon enquired.

"No, of course not—I sent a message—"

"By that jackanapes of a mudlark. Yes, I received it. Very sweet of you to be concerned for my safety. What are we to do with her, Charles?" He asked the question lazily, his brilliant turquoise eyes full of laughter.

"I think that you should escort her down to dinner," the other said. "The gong will be sounding in a moment and then I shall make my entrance."

"Are you a Jacobite then?" Sparrow demanded furiously of Simon as he took her arm and with great ceremony propelled her out into the corridor again. "I don't understand any of this."

"You will learn," he told her, smiling slightly as he kept pace with her along the corridor. Sparrow flung him an exasperated look, but he was gravely handing her down the stairs and there was nothing for her to do at that moment but keep in step.

The guests were already seated as the sonorous note of the dinner gong boomed. The place at the head of the long table was vacant as were several other places.

"Ah, there you are, Mr. Adair." Sir Alasdair spoke heartily as if he and Simon were old friends.

"With another charming addition to your company, Sir Alasdair," Simon said, giving Sparrow a tiny push that seated her abruptly in a vacant chair.

There was nothing for it but to sit there and be quiet. By now she was completely bewildered as to what side Simon Adair was on. She clutched her reticule tightly, trying to take some comfort from the knowledge that her father's pistol, primed and loaded, lay within.

The gong sounded again and those at the table turned their eyes towards the door. Morag opened it with a little flourish and Charles walked in, holding a lady by the hand.

The lady hadn't put on fancy dress or mask but Sparrow would have known her anywhere, even in the deepest disguise.

"My friends, pray allow me to present my sister, Aglaë Roehanstart," Charles said. "She and I have not met for many months until today, and it gives me pleasure to be with her again."

As he escorted her to the head of the table Sparrow, catching Simon's eye, dropped her own gaze hastily. It was absolutely nothing to her if Simon Adair's mistress was also the sister of the Jacobite king.

There were murmurs of surprise and approbation round the table. The lady inclined her head gravely and sat down at her brother's right hand.

Morag and Mrs. Og, the latter clad in a lovely skirt of bright tartan, began to bring in the food. Sparrow had decided that she would not be able to eat a morsel but the smell and sight of the repast mastered her objections and she found herself eating as heartily as the rest.

Yet even as the table conversation circulated with the wine she was conscious of a strain in the atmosphere. Sir Alasdair several times rose from his place and went to look out of the window into the darkening grounds and then sat down again, while those guests who were not engaged in the trivialities of chatter wore uneasy expressions. There were not forty-five present either. Counting the vacant places Sparrow calculated that no more were gathered than thirty including herself. The dreadful suspicion that the arrests for treason had already commenced gripped her.

"To the king over the water," Sir Alasdair said, rising with his glass in his hand. "No, my friends and neighbours, I give you the king who is come into his own again. King Charles the—"

"You go too fast, Sir Alasdair," Charles interrupted from his place of honour. "I beg of you not to offer any toast until I have made my speech."

"Yes, Your—" Sir Alasdair's florid face became more uneasy as he sat down again.

"My friends." The younger man's voice was calm and pleasant, only a faint tremor betraying some inward nervousness. "My name is Charles Roehanstart and I am the grandson of that bonnie prince who sailed away from his kingdom in that terrible time that followed the defeat at Culloden. All my life I have grown up with the glories of the past as my example. My grandfather died when I was four years old but my mother told me so much about him that there have been times when I could have fancied that I too had been part of that glorious and ill-fated venture."

There was silence now, every eye fixed upon the slim young man in the royal tartan who paused, then resumed, leaning forward in his chair.

"Since that day there have been loyal Jacobites to dream and pray and plan for the restoration of the ancient line, and the rumour that Charlotte, Duchess of Albany had legally proved her legitimacy and was herself legally wed found ready listeners. I myself was among them. I too dreamed of the moment when I could proclaim myself as your rightful king. And then the chance came to turn that dream into reality and I was persuaded to travel to Scotland. I was told the clans would rise again and we would achieve what my grandfather failed to achieve. For three months I have waited here, my identity known by some, guessed at by others, and now I have a question to ask you. Where are the clans? Where are the men who come with pipes and claymores to follow their monarch? I hear no marching feet, no cries of battle."

"He's right," Sparrow thought bleakly. "The gentlemen here are nearly all elderly, and there are no pipes and drums."

"Let one clan venture and the rest will join," Sir Alasdair said defiantly.

"And if all the clans were here," Charles said, "it would avail nothing because I have no claim to the Stuart throne."

"You are not Bonnie Prince Charlie's grandson?" Lady Agnes said tremulously.

"My brother and I are both grandchildren of the Prince," Aglaë said, speaking for the first time. "However, these last months, I have been searching in the archives of the Vatican for proof both of my mother's and my grandparents' marriages. There is none. My mother was never legally wed to Cardinal Roehanstart—such an alliance could never have been permitted—and my grandfather never married Clementina Walkinshaw. That was a fiction she invented when he sent for her to join him on the Continent. It made it easier for her to leave her family. It was never more than a defence for herself against humiliation, for the truth was hard for her to bear. In the end she was glad there was no marriage for she was unjustly treated by the Prince and so left him. Charles and I and our sister are illegitimate in two generations and we none of us have any valid claim to any crown anywhere. That is what I came to tell my brother today, for I feared he would be persuaded by your loyalty to our line into an act of treason against the King."

She finished speaking into a silence heavy with disappointed hopes. Then from the end of the table a masked lady said in the voice of the Widow Mackintosh, "But I brought the glove."

"Madam, in blood I am royal," Charles said, "but not in law. If you will do me the honour I will accept the glove as a token of respect for the memory of my grandfather who, when loyal Jacobites gather, will always be Bonnie Prince Charlie."

"And if the clans do come?" Sir Alasdair said.

"Sir, they will not," Simon told him. "Aglaë and I came to inform her brother that there are no grounds for his claim to the throne, and in their hearts the majority know this. They will not come and those who are here ought to thank Providence for it, because the last thing these islands need is another Jacobite rebellion."

He spoke more gravely than Sparrow had ever heard him speak.

"So it is all finished then?" Sir Alasdair sounded as fretful as a child.

"No, sir," Simon said gently. "You cannot kill a dream of chivalry or destroy the bright memory of a gallant enterprise."

"Then we shall drink the toast," the laird said, fumbling to his feet. "To the king over the water and to his descendants wherever they be."

The company was rising, lifting glasses, and the door was opening. With a horrified fascination Sparrow beheld the crumpled skirts and tangled hair of the young woman she had left locked up in the keep.

There was no time to plan anything. She opened her reticule and drew out the pistol, the weight of it heavy and deadly in her small hands.

"Marie!" Charles gave a startled cry as the other advanced into the room.

"I do not enjoy being locked up and having to risk my neck by climbing down the ivy!" Marie's voice was shrill, and a long scratch down one cheek added to her appearance of dishevellment. "I have something for you from King George." She was fumbling in her skirt.

Sparrow caught the gleam of metal and drew her own pistol. She closed her eyes, hearing the loud report as she squeezed the trigger, the acrid scent of gunpowder rising to her nostrils. Someone shouted and there was the crashing of glass.

Opening her eyes she looked down stupidly at the pistol in her hand and then up into Simon's face. He was white beneath his tan and a thin stream of scarlet trickled through the fingers of the hand he held to his shoulder.

"I do believe that I have shot the wrong person," Sparrow said faintly.

And, for the first time in her life, fainted dead away, green skirts billowing round her.

== 14 ==

"YOU ARE THE world's worst shot," Simon said.

His voice came from somewhere over her head. Sparrow opened her eyes cautiously, sneezing as someone else waved burnt feathers under her nose. She wondered if the feathers belonged to Aglaë.

She herself was lying on the sofa in the drawing-room and Simon stood at a little distance, a sling neatly binding his left arm. There were others in the room but at that moment she saw only him.

"I fainted," she informed him unnecessarily.

"You were insensible for quite a considerable period, my dear young lady," Sir Alasdair said.

"Shock following on the heels of influenza," Lady Agnes opined.

"I thought," said Sparrow, raising herself cautiously on her elbow and shaking her head to clear it of dizziness, "that I had killed you."

"A mere graze," Simon assured her. "Where the devil did you obtain the pistol?"

"My father gave it to me as a protection against highwaymen," Sparrow explained.

Lady Agnes put a glass of wine in her hand and she sipped at the sparkling liquid.

"Milord Albany thought that you were a government agent after all for a moment or so," Sir Alasdair said.

"No, Marie Sinclair is the agent," Sparrow demurred. "I lured her to the keep and locked her in. I thought that she and Simon and. . .who is Milord Albany?"

"That is Charles Roehanstart's official title," Simon told her.

"And that other—Aglaë really is his sister?"

"His elder sister. She was raised in France. She and her brother have seldom met in recent years. Aglaë wished to contact him again in order to impress upon him the folly of trying to start a rebellion when he has no legal claim to any throne. Unfortunately, he was moving about incognito and it was some time before she picked up his trail."

"And you have been helping her?"

"Naturally," Simon said, seating himself on the arm of an adjacent chair. "Aglaë is one of my oldest and dearest friends. I knew both her and Charles when I travelled on the Continent."

"Where are they now?" she asked. "And Marie Sinclair? I hope she was disarmed."

"Disarmed?'" he queried.

"She was bringing out a gun," Sparrow said with decision. "I meant to—to deflect her aim."

"You do leap to conclusions, don't you?" Simon said admiringly. "It must be extremely tiring for you."

"Don't you laugh at me, Mr. Adair," she began, but Lady Agnes broke in as a gong sounded elsewhere in the house.

"We must go across to the keep. Mr. Adair, Sparrow, are you both feeling better?"

"I feel perfectly fit," Simon assured her. "Sparrow?"

"So do I," Sparrow said firmly, "but I still don't understand what's—"

"To the keep then," Simon said. "I imagine that Charles is delighted with the plans you have made for his reception."

"We wanted to make it as kingly as possible," Lady Agnes said. "It was all going to be a surprise but now that the clans are not coming—" She signed deeply.

Sparrow, testing her legs, found them reasonably steady and moved out with the others. It was a curious little procession that wended its way out of the side door and through the herb garden. Sir Alasdair led the way with as much determination in his face as if he were leading a charge at Culloden while Lady Agnes, the night wind spraying white powder from her hair over the lantern she had taken up, swayed after him in her enormous hooped skirts. Simon walked at Sparrow's side, and she had the impression, doubtless erroneous, that he was waiting for her to stumble so that he could hold her hand. Two or three of the gentleman guests trailed after, glasses still in their hands.

The slit windows of the keep glowed with soft light and the door was open. No doubt there was another key, Sparrow decided, following the others meekly up the stairs.

The heavy curtains had been drawn back and Charles was seated on the thronelike chair with Aglaë seated in another and Marie Sinclair standing by her, looking as if she had every right to be there. The other guests stood and sat about and there was a lively hum of conversation.

"My dear Miss Sparrow, are you feeling better?" Charles enquired solicitously. "You fainted dead away, you know."

"You don't enquire after me," Simon said with a grin. "I was the one who was shot, you know."

"I've seen you worse hurt in the hunting field," Charles said. "The little lady's aim was not terribly accurate."

"For which we must be profoundly grateful," Simon said dryly. "So you are Marie Sinclair?"

He addressed the brown-haired young woman, who immediately stepped forward, holding out her hand with a cordial, "And you are Milord Albany's old friend, Simon Adair. I am happy to make your acquaintance."

She need not have sounded quite so happy about it, Sparrow thought sourly, and was ashamed of herself as Simon, shaking hands briefly, answered "Well, you led us a pretty chase, Miss Sinclair, and now it seems the chase was unnecessary. Milord stands in no danger of arrest."

"Nor ever did," Marie replied.

"I do wish," said Sparrow plaintively, "that somebody would explain."

"Milord Albany was persuaded by certain Jacobites to return to his ancestors' home," Sir Alasdair said. "I must confess I was convinced that he was of the legitimate line of the royal Stuarts. He agreed at last to come but ventured first into England."

"Wishing to see for myself the country my grandfather had not succeeded in winning," Charles said. "I used the name of Adam Stuart, which had been the name of Sir Alasdair's great-nephew. I met Marie Sinclair and—paid her certain attentions."

"Made violent love to me," corrected that young lady, "though I admit not without encouragement. He confided that he was a Jacobite and even gave me a handkerchief with the emblem of his society embroidered upon it. Then I was approached by a gentleman from the government who told me that it was suspected the Pretender's grandson was in London, and had been seen in my company. So I was asked to arrange a meeting. But Adam—Charles I ought to say—must have guessed that I knew his identity for he disappeared. He thought me a spy, I imagine. He had told me that his great-uncle lived at Craig Bothwell, but I did not repeat that to the gentleman from the government since I feared what they planned to do if they laid hands on him. And I could not follow him openly because they might follow me."

"So you tricked me into coming," Sparrow said indignantly.

"You said that you needed the employment," Marie Sinclair said.

"Which is where Aglaë and I came in," Simon said. "She had come seeking her brother to dissuade him from a venture that was both reckless and illegal, and she naturally contacted me. She had heard that he had taken up with a young woman who had been seen in the company of a government agent, and we were concerned to find and prevent the mischief before Charles was apprehended. When Sparrow dropped the handkerchief I suspected that she might be the young lady, especially since she had already given conflicting reasons for her journey into Scotland. I waited and then we located Marie Sinclair herself who was travelling up to Craig Bothwell on the same stage as Aglaë and myself. We did not tell her the full story since there was always the chance that her motives for finding him were not those she had given to us."

"What a suspicious nature you have," Sparrow couldn't help remarking.

"When we reached Craig Bothwell," Simon continued, ignoring the remark, "Aglaë and I thought it better to go softly, to find out exactly what was being planned before we informed Charles or the Stuarts of our arrival. We made contact with Morag, who showed us all the preparations being made for the proclamation of the new Stuart king."

"That was gravely disloyal of you," Lady Agnes reproached, but Morag drew herself up proudly as she replied, "I'm loyal enough, My Lady, but I know the sorrow that came after Culloden to this house and others. I wasn't happy to be lending my support to a venture that would ruin the family whom my parents and I serve."

"A young woman of excellent sense," Simon approved. "I may propose marriage to you yet."

"That you'd not," she said calmly, "and I'd not accept. Her ladyship knows there's been no man in my heart since the accident that took Adam from us—nor ever will be."

"Meanwhile I was completely at a loss as to what to do," Marie Sinclair said. "Neither Mr. Adair nor the Lady Aglaë had taken me fully into their confidence. They feared I meant to betray Charles, and I feared they meant to lend their support to an uprising in the Jacobite Cause. I decided to try to see myself, to give him what was entrusted to me to bring him." There was the same gleam of metal that Sparrow had glimpsed before as Marie drew a thin silver box from the deep pocket in her skirts.

"His Royal Highness the Prince Regent wished this to be given to you, Milord Albany," she said formally. "He wishes me to tell you that he has taken this step without the official sanction of his Council, but he begs you will receive it in the spirit of reconciliation with which it is offered."

She sank into a graceful curtsey and handed the box to Charles.

All conversation had ceased long since, every guest listening intently to the sequence of events now being unfolded. Charles lifted the lid and drew out the rolled document within. "It is the offer of a pension to be paid regularly out of the Prince Regent's own purse," Marie said breathlessly, "on the condition that Milord Albany does not seek to establish himself as a legitimate claimant to the throne."

"It's a generous offer," he said slowly, raising his fair head from the paper.

"Will you take it?" Aglaë asked.

Beyond the walls of the chamber in which they were clustered a sound pierced a stone. A high, skirling sound, sweet as forgotten dreams, its theme taken up by others above the jangle of harness and the tramp of marching feet.

"The clans are coming," Sir Alasdair said. "Didn't I tell you they'd be here?"

In the dark beyond the arrow-slit windows points of light streamed into fire and the sound of the pipes grew louder and wilder.

"Will you proclaim our right to the throne?" Lady Agnes asked eagerly. "There might still be proof of the marriages."

She wanted there to be proof, Sparrow thought. She wanted, as always, to turn back the clock.

"There are at least three hundred men coming." Sir Alasdair had moved to the window. "Your grandfather started out with less. Others would join once the standard was raised."

"For me to lead to another Culloden?" Charles's voice was wry. "No, my friends, that is not the path for any of us to take."

"You will accept the pension?" Aglaë said.

"I will accept it," he answered gravely, "but first I will go down and thank them for their loyalty to my family. Can they be accommodated and fed?"

"The villagers made preparations," Lady Agnes told him.

He had risen, bowing to the company, taking his sister's hand as he left the chamber.

"He has not the stomach for it after all," one of the gentlemen said in a disappointed tone.

"On the contrary, sir," Simon retorted, "I have never seen him with more of his grandfather's gallantry in him. He might have made a fine king had his birth been legitimate."

"Perhaps we should go down," Lady Agnes suggested. "There is still the ball. Miss Sinclair, you are very welcome to make one of the party."

"That's very kind of you, Lady Agnes. I shall come as a kitchen maid," Marie said ruefully.

"And I will go and pack," Sparrow said with sudden resolution. "Lady Agnes, I have to tell you that I am not—"

"Not the replacement for Miss Marchmont? Oh, I know that already, my dear," Lady Agnes said calmly. "There was a letter come by the last stage to apologise because the young lady had decided that Scotland was too far to come for a short time."

"And you never said anything? You didn't confront me?" Sparrow stared at her.

"It did occur to me that you might be running away from someone or other," Lady Agnes said.

"I might have been a government agent," Sparrow said. "Mr. Adair suspected that I was."

"My own mind," said Lady Agnes loftily, sweeping after her husband, "does not run on those lines, my dear Sparrow, and never will. Miss Sinclair."

"He really was rather splendid, wasn't he?" Marie lingered to say. "You know, I was never much in love with him before, but now I think I might make more progress."

"The pension helping," Simon said.

"Naturally." She shot him an amused look. "A young woman must consider her chief interests."

They were leaving the keep with the chamber that had been prepared for a king in exile and streaming back through the herb garden to the brightly lit house. Sparrow made to follow them but Simon caught her arm.

"What mischief are you contemplating now?" he demanded.

"I never do contemplate it," she said haughtily, "but it has a habit of rushing upon me unaware. Now, if you will excuse me, I shall thank the Stuarts for their great kindness and hear Peter recite his poem, which he has been at very great pains to con, and then I will—"

"Do what?" he enquired.

"I shall return to London," she answered. "There is a stage and I have money for it. You need not concern yourself with my welfare in the least."

"Oh, I don't," he said promptly. "Not in the least. I never yet met a young lady more capable of looking after herself. You are quite astonishingly versatile."

"And I daresay that Lady Aglaë will be occupying your attention anyway," Sparrow said.

"Why should she? Ah, you think that she and I—" His boyish grin lifted the craggy sternness of his features and his blue eyes danced. "We have been friends for years, of course."

"You embraced her," slipped from Sparrow's lips before she could prevent it.

"On the Continent embraces are frequent between old friends, as are terms of endearment. I am hoping that you are jealous, or is your heart still in the keeping of the estimable Henry?"

"As a matter of fact Charles—the Prince was inclined to admire me," she told him.

"Then you had better hurry back to the ball," Simon said. "I fancy that Miss Sinclair has decided to capture him after all. She is a young lady who will never let her heart rule her head."

"Then we have something in common."

"Yes indeed," he mused. "You would never dream of turning down a proposal of marriage from a most eligible gentleman because you knew he did not love you, nor of taking a grubby mudlark under your wing, nor of telling lies to spare your relatives pain and anxiety, nor of shooting someone in defence of someone else."

"I think," Sparrow said thoughtfully, "that I will take a course of instruction before I attempt to use firearms again."

"Very wise, my dear Sparrow. And whom are you planning to shoot next?"

"I have already apologised for that," Sparrow said crossly. "I really am very relieved that I didn't kill you, but if you continue to tease me I shall begin to wish I had hit a little closer."

"So you will travel back to London?" He was between her and the door. "Your father is deep in debt, is he not? The excellent Mrs. O'Hara was moved to confide in me to a certain extent."

"My father's luck will change," Sparrow said. "It always does. Meanwhile I shall contrive to make a living."

"I have an idea," he said.

"If you are contemplating a proposal in order to safeguard my financial future then I must remind you that I have already rejected Henry."

"I wasn't thinking of proposing," Simon said blandly.

"Oh," said Sparrow. "Well, that's perfectly splendid then. Perfectly splendid. Shall we go and—?"

"I was thinking of a partnership to our mutual financial benefit," Simon informed her.

"What sort of partnership?" Sparrow asked suspiciously.

"Well, it occurs to me that you have a positive genius for involving yourself in the affairs of other people," he said, "and I also seem to become embroiled in affairs that are not directly my concern. Perhaps we ought to join forces? Advertise ourselves as problem-solvers extraordinary."

"I never heard of such a thing," Sparrow said blankly.

"Neither did I, but there's no reason why such a profession cannot be invented," he returned. "Husbands leave their wives, ladies lose their jewellery, young gentleman get into debt and require extricating—a discreet personal service guaranteed to help anyone in a predicament sounds splendid to me."

"Sparrow and Simon?" she said uncertainly.

"By all means let the lady come first," he said.

"The whole idea is preposterous," she said firmly. "I am not a person who deliberately seeks out trouble, you know. This whole affair has wearied me out."

"Then as you are too tired to dance you will not object to sitting out with me," he bowed. "I am incapacitated by my wound."

"Graze."

'I was being brave about it," he said.

"Oh, Simon, you are a fool," Sparrow said, breaking into sudden laughter.

"And you," he returned, circling her slender waist with his free hand, "are completely and utterly enchanting."

Sparrow had time for one startled "Oh" before his mouth demanded a different response. It was not, she thought in happy confusion, in the least like being kissed by Henry, who had never done more than peck at her cheek.

"You ought not—you have not proposed marriage," she said breathlessly at last.

"I haven't any money," Simon said simply. "Also, I may be desperately in love with you but it will take me several months to adjust to the fact before I even begin to think of settling down. Perhaps we should postpone an official announcement until Sparrow and Simon, Advisers and Investigators, is more firmly established?"

"Would anyone hire us, do you think?" Her arms round his neck, she asked the question with a smile matching his own at the back of her eyes.

"If they are completely crazy," Simon said, and kissed her again.

"Let 'er alone." Running feet up the staircase and Lance burst in, his expression indignant.

"What on earth are you doing here?" Simon demanded. "I left you at the tavern."

"So you could sneak back and 'ave your will," Lance said truculently. "You did say as 'ow I was supposed to rescue you, Miss."

"Only when I need rescuing," Sparrow said. "Mr. Adair and I were—were signing a business agreement."

"Does that mean we're all going 'ome?" Lance demanded.

"I imagine it does," Simon said, "since I see that if I take Miss Sparrow as a partner you will insist on coming along too, though I can't think what capacity you can fill."

"He can run errands," Sparrow said.

"And rescue ladies like you said?" Lance said eagerly.

"Only when they need it," Sparrow said firmly. "Now go on down to the kitchen quarters and tell Morag, the maid-servant there, that you are a friend of mine and require some refreshment."

"You mean ask for vittles?" Lance regarded the two of them shrewdly. "What are you going to be doing?"

"Discussing business affairs. Out." Simon emphasised the command with a jerk of the head.

"It is really very good of you to consider taking the boy on," Sparrow said as Lance ran down the stairs again.

"It's very good of me to consider taking you on," Simon retorted. "I have no doubts that our partnership will be bedevilled by mudlarks, fathers with broken legs, and red-headed imps who leap into trouble without thinking."

"If that last referred to me, then it wasn't very polite," Sparrow reproached.

"Then let us be formal and polite by all means. Miss Harvey, will you consider becoming my business partner with a definite view to a more intimate partnership later?"

"Mr. Adair, I must be quite out of my mind to consider such an offer," she answered gravely, "but the truth is that I would like nothing better in the whole world."

"There's only one answer to that," Simon said.

And made it, while the skirling of the bagpipes came from the brightly lit house, and all the dreams of the past were swallowed up in hopes for the future.

If you would like to receive details of other Walker Regency Romances, send for your free subscription to our Walker Regency Newsletter,

"The Season"
Regency Editor
Walker and Company
720 Fifth Avenue
New York, NY 10019